SYNOPSIS

Neil Watkins isn't too surprised to receive an invitation to Rob Asher and Ben Rockingham's wedding. After all, he's been best friends with Ben's son Kyle for several years. But he is excited to be invited to join them on the honeymoon - a party for a select group of family and friends on an all-expense paid Mediterranean cruise. He's hesitant at first, but Kyle convinces him to go. Well, his own love life sucks at the moment. Maybe he'll have better luck in the Med.

When he receives an invitation to their wedding and honeymoon party, Matthew Palmer balks at the idea of joining Rob and Ben on their honeymoon cruise. The master jeweler, a friend to both men, thinks the offer is way too generous, but Rob's best friend Samantha persuades him to rethink his decision. His last relationship really knocked him for a loop, and maybe Sam was right and he should think about himself for a change.

When Neil and Matthew meet, unexpected and undeniable sparks fly. Has their luck finally changed? Can this really be their second chance at love in the Mediterranean?

Love on the Potomac

NEW ADVENTURES IN LOVE · BOOK 3

RJ Peterson

Love in the Mediterranean

New Adventures in Love, Book 4

Copyright © 2022 by R.J. Peterson

Cover design & interior design and formatting by Ron Perry Graphic Design, rperrydesign.com

Cover content is for illustrative purposes only. Any person depicted on the cover is a model. Cover background photography by Ron Perry.

Editing by Lyrical Lines, lyricallines.net

Proofreading by Lisa Lakeland, LesCourt Author Services, lescourtauthorservices.com

Digital ISBN: 978-1-967317-06-6

Print ISBN: 978-1-967317-17-2

This novel contains mature sexual content. Reader discretion is advised.

No Generative AI Training Use.

For avoidance of doubt, Author reserves the rights, and does not grant permission to any individual/company/publisher/platform any rights to reproduce and/or otherwise use the Work in any manner for purposes of training artificial intelligence technologies to generate text, including without limitation, technologies that are capable of generating works in the same style or genre as the Work, unless said individual/company/publisher/platform obtains Author's specific and express permission to do so. Nor does any individual/company/publisher/platform have the right to sublicense others to reproduce and/or otherwise use the Work in any manner for purposes of training artificial intelligence technologies to generate text without Author's specific and express permission.

In addition, no artificial intelligence (A.I.), predictive language software, or generative design software was used in any part of the creation of this book or its cover, nor will it ever be for any of my works.

To Sammi Cee

Author, friend, and all around amazing person.
I'm a better writer because of you.

Thank you.

"There are good ships and wood ships, ships that sail the sea,
but the best ships are friendships, may they always be."

- Irish Proverb

CONTENTS

A WORD ABOUT COVID

When I wrote my first book, *Love On The Horizon*, I wasn't expecting it to become a series, so I purposely set it in the fall of 2019, thus avoiding any reference to COVID-19. But then, something interesting happened...

As I continued to write that first book, I started to get ideas for additional stories in the same universe. Once I published *Love On The Horizon*, I started working on book two and made a decision. The New Adventures in Love series all happens in a parallel universe that is exactly like the world we live in—except there's no COVID pandemic.

We've all suffered enough in so many ways over the past few years. I thought it might be nice for this series to be an escape from all that.

Acknowledgments

This book is, in so many ways, a group effort…

David, my husband, friend, and travel partner. Thanks for your support and for continuing to make me laugh for 42+ years. Here's to new adventures and many more laughs!

My alpha & beta readers – Sammi, Karen, & Mia, and my editor Dianne and proofreader Lisa, this book is so much better thanks to your guidance and input. I couldn't have done it without all of you.

Sharon, K-lee, Melissa, Teresa, Tal, Greg, Hank, Meredith, Annabella, Ann, and so many more – the word 'thanks' seems inadequate, but it's the only one I've got at the moment. Your belief in me and my writing helps me get through the day.

Special thanks to Shona, Lucy, Cheryl, Betty, Bernadette, Ana, Shaz, & Darlene for providing a list of various nautical names and terms that I've been able to use when naming public rooms on my fictional cruise ships in the course of writing this series.

I love you all very much.

PROLOGUE

"I've decided to give up men. Maybe I'll become a priest."

Kyle coughed, almost choking on his martini. "What the fuck, Neil! Don't say shit like that as I'm sipping my drink! You almost wore it. And weren't you raised Methodist; they don't have priests, do they?"

"Priest, minister, tomayto, tomahto. At this point, I have no love life, so celibacy isn't gonna be a problem. I've given up, Kyle. I'm never gonna meet a decent guy. My life sucks."

The two friends were sitting at the bar at Logan Tavern, a favorite spot of theirs not far from their respective homes. They had decided to stop there for a drink and a bite to eat after a long day at the investment firm where they worked.

"I take it your date didn't go so well last night?"

"Ugh. It was awful," Neil admitted. "He was cute but so boring. Apparently, he still lives with his mom. All he could talk about was his collection of banana stickers and all the soap operas he records, then watches with her every night. Ugh."

"His collection of what? What the hell are banana stickers? Wait. Forget I asked. I really don't wanna know."

"You're a smart man, Kyle Rockingham. And you're right. You really don't wanna know." Neil shook his head and sipped his cosmopolitan. "And now, for a complete change of subject, are you excited to see that hot boyfriend of yours?"

Kyle's boyfriend, Jon Rivera, had applied for a job at the law firm where Kyle's uncle worked. The plan was for him to move from his home in Phoenix to DC very soon.

"I am." Kyle sighed, smiling. "He's landing tomorrow morning; he'll take a Lyft right to Mike's firm for his interview. Depending on how things go, he may stop by the office so we can have lunch. You're more than welcome to join us if you'd like."

"Thanks, I'll think about it. I don't normally like being a third wheel, but I haven't seen Jon in a few months, and I really like him, so yeah, maybe I will join you two."

Kyle drank the last of his martini and signaled the bartender.

"Another round, gentlemen?" the bartender asked.

"I'll have a glass of Carménère, please," Kyle replied. "And the Signature Burger, medium."

"I'll have the same," Neil added.

"I know things seem bleak right now, Neil. But mark my words, your luck is gonna change."

"If you say so. But I'm not holding my breath."

The bartender returned with their wine. "The burgers will be up in a few minutes."

"Oh, I just remembered. You'll be getting an invitation to Dad and Rob's wedding. Dad mentioned it to me when we chatted last weekend. He and Rob both like you a lot, and they really want you there. I've already requested my vacation days, but it's still early enough that you shouldn't have any problems getting the time off as well. I think it would do you good to go on a Mediterranean cruise for a couple of weeks."

"Wait, what? Are they really inviting me to the honeymoon party?" Neil replied in disbelief. "I guess I sort of expected to be invited to the wedding, but the honeymoon too? Wow, I still can't believe they're taking a bunch of folks on their honeymoon with them."

"I know, right? But they were adamant about making it a big celebration with family and friends," Kyle said. "Well, they can certainly afford it, and since it's not a first marriage for either of them, the whole 'let's party together' idea really appealed to them."

"So they decided on the cruise, huh? What were their other choices again?" Neil asked.

"Renting a Caribbean island for a week or reserving a castle somewhere in Ireland were both in the running, but since they met in Barcelona and spent a week together on a cruise two years ago, they thought it would be sweet to do that again."

"Well, I don't feel worthy of the invitation, but I promise to think about it."

"Fair enough. But don't wait too long to decide. You still need to get the okay to take time off, and Dad and Rob need an answer pretty quickly so that Sam can get all the arrangements made." Sam was Rob's best friend, Samantha Martinez, a wizard of a travel agent who was handling all the details for the honeymoon.

"You're going to do everything you can to talk me into going, aren't you?" Neil knew his friend all too well. "Remind me how this is all gonna work."

"The way I understand it," Kyle continued, "the wedding will be in the morning, followed by a small reception. That night, those of us who are going on the cruise will all head to Boston for a flight to Barcelona. We'll all stay in a hotel for one night, then the cruise starts the following day and ends twelve days later in Venice. From what Dad told me, the ship actually overnights in Venice, so we'll have time to see some of the city before we fly home the next day."

"Whew." Neil whistled. "So ... two weeks. I don't think I've ever taken a vacation for that long. Let me think about it a bit more, but I promise I'll decide quickly."

Just then, the bartender placed their burgers in front of them. "Enjoy, gentlemen."

NEIL ENTERED his apartment complex lobby and stopped to check his mailbox. Grabbing the envelopes and flyers, he moved toward the elevator and hit the call button. As he waited, he looked through the mail in his hand, and sure enough, there was a heavy white envelope with a Westport return address among the items.

When he got to his apartment, he took a letter opener from the junk drawer in the kitchen and slid it through the envelope flap.

The invitation was simple but beautiful. Navy type in a

classic serif font with a stunning blue watercolor graphic, reminiscent of the ocean, along the bottom of the heavy white panel. Also in the envelope were two RSVP cards—one for the wedding and reception and a second for the honeymoon cruise.

MAYBE KYLE IS RIGHT. I deserve to do something for myself, and maybe this is just what I need to kick-start my nonexistent love life. I can't imagine meeting Mr. Right, but maybe, just maybe, I'll meet Mr. Right Now, and that will be just fine with me.

CHAPTER 1

Matthew was sitting at his worktable in the back room when he heard the bell ring, indicating that the front door to the Artisan Alchemist had opened. A couple of moments later, Christine, the store manager, poked her head through the doorway.

"Hey, Matthew, Rob and Ben are here to see you."

"Thanks, I'll be out in a second," he said, removing the lighted magnifying glasses he wore when working on the fine details that graced some of his custom-design pieces.

He quickly washed his hands and checked his face to make sure there were no stray marks on his dark complexion. Earlier, he'd been sketching a possible design, and he sometimes ended up with graphite or charcoal streaks along his chin or nose. Walking into the main part of the shop, he looked around and smiled. It wasn't overly large, but it was his, and he was extremely proud of it.

Several counters with jewelry cases were arranged symmetrically around the room. Many of the pieces on display had nautical themes—compass rose designs, whale's tail pendants, and lighthouses, mostly in silver or gold. Then there were more abstract pieces, incorporating sea glass along with the precious metals. The shop did a good business in the summer, when tourists were aplenty in town. But Matthew's real love was the custom pieces he designed. That had started out by popular demand from some of the locals but had expanded to a worldwide market when he updated his website to promote the custom-design side of the business.

"Hi Rob, Ben," he greeted them warmly, hugging each man in turn. "Thanks for coming in today; I wanted to show you the designs I've been working on for your wedding rings."

He directed them to a cozy sitting area in the back corner of the store, which contained a small desk and some chairs. "Let's sit over here, and I can show you my ideas."

He opened the desk drawer and pulled out a sketchbook, an iPad Mini, and a small tray containing various objects.

"Since I knew you were coming in, I got this all ready as soon as I came in this morning."

Opening the sketchbook, he flipped to a page and placed it in front of them. "Here are some sketches of what I had in mind."

There were several iterations of a ring, beautifully rendered in black and white, and a few with some added color.

"I really like this one," Ben said, pointing to an asymmetrical-band design with different widths of materials surrounding the ring.

"Yeah, that's gorgeous," Rob agreed. "What are those different materials?"

"Okay, I started with a base of platinum since you both wanted to stay with a silver color to match your bracelets." Matthew had designed the two bracelets that the men wore. They were a combination of platinum and leather, with a clasp in the shape of a compass rose. Rob had commissioned him to design them as a Christmas gift for Ben—including one for himself—last year.

"The wider blue channel is blue opal. It reminded me of the ocean when I was searching for a gemstone to use." He smiled thoughtfully. "I felt that was appropriate considering you met in the Mediterranean." He took a piece of blue opal from the tray so they could see an actual sample.

"That's so cool. I love it," Rob said, awe in his voice. Ben nodded in agreement.

"This thinner channel is oak from a bourbon barrel. As you know, I share your love of bourbon, so that also made sense to me. Finally, the two narrow gray bands are from a meteorite. It didn't really have any significance for the two of you, but I thought the gray tones tied everything together nicely."

"Well, I always say that Rob is outta this world, so I guess that fits too." Ben joked.

Rob groaned but smiled lovingly at his fiancé.

"I have a version on the iPad as well. It's not perfect but might give you a better idea than my sketch." Opening the tablet, he tapped an icon and scrolled a bit, then showed them a beautiful 3D computer rendering of the ring.

"Oh my god!" Rob exclaimed. His voice broke slightly. "It's gorgeous."

Ben grabbed his hand. "Oh, Matthew, you've outdone

yourself. I think it's obvious that we both love it. Right, sweetheart?" He turned to Rob.

"Yes," Rob said quietly. "Let's do this."

"Excellent. I'm so glad you like it. I want to double-check your ring sizes, then I can start on the rings next week. They'll be done long before the wedding, but I don't want to put this off."

He pulled out a set of plain rings in various sizes. Looking first at Rob's ring finger, then Ben's, he chose a couple and had them try the sizer rings on. Rob's fit perfectly, but Ben's was too small, so he went up a half size, and that one worked.

"Do you need a deposit or something, Matthew?" Ben asked.

"Not at all. I know you guys and trust you both," Matthew answered. He gave them a ballpark figure for the pair of rings. "We'll settle up when they're done."

They stood, and Rob pulled an envelope out of his back pocket. "We wanted to deliver this in person, Matthew. You're a good friend, and naturally you're invited to the wedding, but we also want you to join us for the honeymoon party. It's an all-expense-paid Mediterranean cruise that we're doing for our family and some close friends, and we really want you to come."

"I really appreciate it, guys, but I couldn't. It's too much." He knew the shock had to be evident on his face.

"Nonsense," Ben said. "It's October, so you can afford to take some time off. Christine can certainly handle things in the off-season, and you never do anything for yourself."

"I don't know—" Matthew started.

"Promise us you'll at least think about it," Rob pleaded.

"Okay, I promise," Matthew said, not wanting to cause a scene.

They hugged again as Rob and Ben left the shop.

Christine sauntered over to him. From the look on her face, she'd obviously overheard at least part of the conversation. She stared at him pointedly and said, "They're right, you know. You're long overdue for a vacation. And I can definitely handle this place for a couple of weeks. You really need to do this."

"Fine, I'll give it some serious thought." He knew better than to argue with Christine.

MATTHEW ENTERED the bungalow he called home. It wasn't huge, but it was more than enough space for him. Living room, large eat-in kitchen, two bedrooms, and a bathroom that he splurged on with an enormous shower and a separate whirlpool tub. But the home's best feature was that it was located at Westport Point; the large bay window in the living room had panoramic views of the west branch of the Westport River. He could stare at that view forever.

He went to the fridge and poured himself a glass of sauvignon blanc. Sitting on the side deck that also overlooked the river, he took a sip of the cold, crisp wine and tapped the wedding invitation on his knee.

Wow, I can't believe that Rob and Ben actually invited me to go on the cruise with them. I knew they were planning a destination honeymoon party for some of their family and friends, but never in a million years did I expect to be invited. How crazy is that?

The more he thought about it, the more he concluded that

Rob, Ben, and Christine were right. He never did anything for himself. Except for taking a few days off last year when his brother Marcus came to visit him, he hadn't had a vacation in a few years. He and Stephen had still been dating at the time of his last real vacation, so that was at least three years ago. And since his folks didn't really speak to him anymore, he wouldn't take time off to visit them in Nashua. God, he was pathetic. Thirty-seven and single—he couldn't remember the last time he'd been on a date.

The ring of his phone startled him out of his thoughts. A glance at the screen told him it was Rob's friend Samantha calling.

"Hey, Sam," he said cheerfully. "What's up?"

"Hi, Matthew. Can't a friend just call to say hello?"

"Well, sure, but saying it that way, I suspect there's another reason for your call."

"Busted," she admitted. "I spoke to Rob earlier, and he told me that he and Ben stopped by your shop. They both love the design you've come up with for their wedding rings."

"Thanks. They seemed really excited about the sketches and rendering I showed them. I suppose Rob asked you to call me and try to talk me into going on the cruise, right?"

"Wow, it's like you know him," she uttered, laughing. "But he's not wrong, Matthew. You deserve something like this. I don't think you've gone anywhere since you and Stephen broke up. You don't even visit your family in New Hampshire anymore."

Sam, Rob, and Ben were probably the only people Matthew opened up to. Rob and Sam were around when things fell apart with Stephen, and he was able to lean on both of them for support while he got over his ex.

And the three of them had been there for him last year when he had the blowout with his parents. He'd come out to them several years ago when he moved to Westport; they'd not taken the news well. His parents had joined an evangelical Christian church and were not happy with the news that their son was gay. At the time, it had become a topic they avoided talking about, but last year, his folks, well, his dad especially, started talking about conversion therapy, and Matthew stopped talking to them altogether. He still spoke to his two brothers once in a while, but he just couldn't deal with the vitriol that his dad spewed about his lifestyle.

"You know I can't deal with my folks," he said, feeling agitated. "So what's the point of driving to Nashua? Mom's not so bad although she keeps telling me that she's praying for my soul, but Dad is relentless." He paused, trying to calm himself. "Sorry, Sam, I didn't mean to get upset."

"No apologies necessary, Matthew. I know it's a sore subject with you, and I didn't mean to cause you grief. You still talk to Marcus and Micah, though, right?" she asked, inquiring about his brothers.

"Yeah, we manage to talk every week or two. And they keep me updated on Mom and Dad, so I know they're both okay even if they think I'm damned to hell forever." Matthew chuckled sadly. "I keep hoping they'll come around, but I just don't see it happening anytime soon."

"Well, that's even more of a reason to consider this cruise. Rob and Ben really want you there, and I do too. We'll have lots of fun, and you can forget about family for a couple of weeks. And who knows, maybe someone will catch your eye."

"Ha, I doubt I'll meet anyone, but okay. Message received. I'm not one hundred percent committed yet, but I'm a lot closer to saying yes than I was earlier today. Thanks for calling and trying to convince me, Sam. I really don't know what I'd do without friends like you and Rob and now Ben."

"Well, then, my work here is done—at least for now. And you know you can always depend on us to support you. We're family, Matthew."

"Thanks, Sam. Okay. I'm gonna go make some dinner. I'll talk to you later."

"Bye."

Sam's right; I should go on this cruise. I can unwind and be myself. I probably won't meet anyone, because I don't have that kind of luck, but the change of scenery will do me good. Perhaps I can get some inspiration for some new jewelry designs. Okay, I'll do it!

CHAPTER 2

The alarm on his iPhone was ringing as Neil slowly opened his eyes. Reaching over to the nightstand, he shut it off. The surroundings were unfamiliar, and it took him a moment to get his bearings. Ah, yes, he was in his room at the bed-and-breakfast that Ben and Rob had reserved for him. Their wedding was today! Neil needed to get his butt in gear since a van was picking him and a few others up in a little over an hour.

He showered and pulled out his clothes for the wedding. Since they'd both been married before, Ben and Rob had decided to keep this celebration informal. Neil had chosen navy slacks, a pale-blue open-collared shirt, and a tweed sports jacket with flecks of brown, tan, and navy. Once he was ready, he went downstairs to grab some breakfast. When he got to the dining room, he saw that Ben's brother Mike and his wife, Ellen, along with Mike Jr., his wife, Becky, and their one-year-old son, Wyatt, were seated at a large round table.

"Hey, Neil, come sit with us." Mike waved him over.

Neil had met Mike and Ellen on a few different occasions in DC, but he'd just met Mike Jr., Becky, and their son yesterday when they arrived at the B&B.

"Thanks, Mike. Good morning, everyone."

"Would you like some coffee, Neil?" Ellen picked up the carafe on the table.

"Yes, please."

Anthony, the owner of the bed-and-breakfast, walked up to the table. "Good morning, Mr. Watkins. We have a buffet set up for breakfast; if there's anything else you'd like, please let me know."

"Thank you, I'm sure the buffet will be fine. I need this coffee more than anything else."

Mike Jr. chuckled. "I know what you mean. But I highly recommend the breakfast casserole. It's delicious."

Anthony departed, and Neil went to the buffet to grab some food.

When he returned, Mike said, "I spoke to Ben this morning. He sounded a bit nervous, but he said he was really excited to finally marry Rob. I'm very happy they found each other."

Conversation turned to more mundane things, and before they knew it, Anthony walked back into the dining room and addressed their table.

"Excuse me, everyone. Are you ready to go? Your driver is here."

"Yeah, I believe we are," Mike replied. "C'mon, people, we've got a wedding to attend."

WHEN THEY ARRIVED at Ben and Rob's home, Sam led Neil into the kitchen so that he could see Kyle and Jon before the ceremony.

Kyle hugged Neil tightly. "I'm sorry we weren't able to spend time with you last night, but it got a bit crazy here with some last-minute preparations."

"No worries, Kyle. I totally understand. I got to spend some time with Mike and Ellen and their family at the B&B. It's all good."

Jon came over and gave Neil a hug. "I'm so glad you're here, Neil."

"So, is there anything I can do to help? Is everything under control?"

Jon turned to Kyle and pinned a boutonniere on the lapel of his navy jacket. It was a small deep-purple iris with some greenery and nicely complemented his lavender shirt. Tan chinos completed his outfit.

Kyle glanced at his watch. "Actually, if you can find Sam and ask her to come in here, I'd really appreciate it. We should be starting in about fifteen minutes. I think she may have gone out to the deck."

"Sure, I'll take care of it."

Neil exited the kitchen and looked around the top floor of the multilevel deck on the back of the house. Even though it was a beautiful fall day, there were several propane heaters scattered around the deck to ward off any autumn chill that might occur. Buffet tables were set up along the outside wall of the house, and the rest of the space contained some small tables and chairs. Neil assumed the reception would take place here later.

He could see folks gathered in small groups on the next level down, so he descended the stairs in search of Sam.

There were roughly thirty people mingling throughout the space, and he saw Sam at one end standing next to a tall, striking woman with a halo of gray curls. She was clad in judge's robes, and Neil guessed she'd be officiating at the ceremony. He approached them, admiring Sam's eggplant-hued dress and matching pumps. Her hair was pulled up to the side and featured tiny lavender irises and some pale-green ribbons.

"Excuse me, Sam," Neil began. "Kyle would like you in the house as they'll be ready to start in a few minutes."

"Of course. Neil, this is Judge Marjorie Sampson. She'll be officiating today. Marjorie, this is Neil Watkins, Kyle's best friend from DC."

Sam excused herself and walked away.

"Pleased to meet you, Judge Sampson."

"You as well. And please call me Marjorie."

"Do you know Rob and Ben well?" Neil asked.

"I've known Rob for many years and have gotten to know Ben better in the past several months. I'm so very happy that they met. Rob was devastated when his first husband, Alan, died suddenly several years ago. I wasn't sure he would survive that."

"I've known Ben for a while, and Kyle says he's never seen his dad happier, so it seems like their meeting has been great for both of them."

Something captured Marjorie's attention, and Neil turned

to see what she was looking at. He saw Sam and Kyle on the upper deck. Kyle nodded to a DJ in the corner, and a piano arrangement of "Wind Beneath My Wings" could be heard coming through a few strategically placed speakers.

Sam and Kyle descended the stairs, followed by Rob and Ben, hand in hand. The two handsome men were dressed in tan chinos and navy blazers, with deep-eggplant-colored shirts open at the collar. A small lavender iris was pinned to each of their lapels.

Neil discreetly moved aside so that the couple could stand in front of Judge Sampson, with Sam on Rob's left and Kyle on Ben's right.

As the song ended, Marjorie began speaking.

"Friends and loved ones, we gather together today to celebrate the love between these two men. Rob and Ben have asked us to witness their commitment to each other."

As she nodded to Rob, a quiet, instrumental arrangement of "I Will Always Love You" began to play softly in the background.

"Ben, I promise to always care for you, comfort you, and celebrate with you. I will be by your side through whatever life may throw at us and will cherish the time we have together. You entered my life when I was so very fragile, and you loved me for who I was. You made me whole again when I didn't think that was possible. I can't wait to continue this adventure with you. I love you with all my heart." Rob's voice quavered a bit, and his eyes were bright with unshed tears.

Marjorie smiled and turned to Ben, nodding once again.

"Rob, I will be your comrade in adventure, your accomplice in mischief, your comfort in disappointment, your strength in times of need, and your partner in all things, for all the days of my life. I'm so lucky to have found someone who embraces all that I am and enriches my life in so many ways, and I'm excited for what the future holds for us. I promise to love you forever." Ben's voice was steady, his actor's training clearly kicking in.

"Rob and Ben, you've promised to love and care for each other forever. And so I ask, Robert Asher, do you take Ben to be your husband?"

"I do."

"And Bentley Rockingham, do you take Rob to be your husband?"

"I most certainly do."

"Do you have the rings?"

Sam and Kyle each handed a ring to Rob and Ben, who then held them in front of the judge.

"The ring is an age-old symbol of timelessness, unity, and eternity. May it represent your love and a very long life together. Rob, please place the ring on Ben's finger and repeat after me, 'Ben, with this ring, I thee wed.'"

"Ben, with this ring, I thee wed." Rob's voice was quiet, almost reverent.

"Now Ben, please place the ring on Rob's finger and repeat after me, 'Rob, with this ring, I thee wed.'"

Ben took a breath, placed the ring on Rob's finger, and staring into his eyes, said, "Rob, with this ring, I thee wed."

"What love has brought together today, let no one break apart. By the power vested in me by the Commonwealth of Massachusetts, I pronounce you married. Gentlemen, you may kiss your husband."

As they kissed, gently at first, then with a little more heat, the crown applauded.

Neil glanced over at Sam and saw her wiping her eyes. As he looked toward Kyle, he noticed that he was doing the same.

Ben took his husband's hand and turned toward the group of friends and family surrounding them.

"Thank you all for being here with us today. It means so much to us that you're here to celebrate our marriage. Now let's get this party started. Enjoy!" He raised their joined hands, and then they kissed again as "Celebration" by Kool & the Gang could be heard through the sound system.

AS THE CEREMONY ENDED, Neil looked around for a familiar face. Sam and Kyle were with Ben, Rob, and the photographer, so he scanned the crowd for Jon. Aside from Ben's family, he assumed that most of the crowd was made up of friends and neighbors of the grooms. Spotting Jon on the other side of the deck, chatting with someone whose back was turned to him, Neil headed that way.

"Hey, Jon," Neil said as he approached.

"Hi, Neil. I'd like you to meet Matthew Palmer. Matthew, this is Neil Watkins, Kyle's best friend from DC."

Matthew was almost as tall as Neil, with a swimmer's build, his skin a deep sepia brown. His dark hair was close-cropped, and he gazed at Neil with bright, golden-brown eyes. As they shook hands, Neil felt a spark of something indefinable. *Who was this man?*

"Nice to meet you, Neil."

"I, um, yeah. Same. I mean, nice to meet you too." *Oh my god, he must think I'm an idiot! Breathe. You can do this.* "Sorry, I'm just a little overwhelmed by the day ... I think. Usually my mouth works better than this." *Oh, fuck, what did I just say? God, kill me now!*

Matthew chuckled, his eyes sparkling. "No worries, I think we're all a bit emotional today. It was a beautiful ceremony for two really great guys."

"Neil, Matthew is the jeweler who designed the rings for Ben and Rob."

"Oh, you designed their bracelets too, didn't you? I remember Kyle telling me about them. I finally got a chance to see them earlier this year when Ben and Rob were in DC to visit Kyle. They're beautiful."

"Thank you. Yes, I created the bracelets for them; they were a bit challenging but also a lot of fun to design."

"I'll need to get a closer look at the rings. You're very talented, Matthew. I know Ben's only been around for a little while, but have you known Rob very long?" Neil was finally calming down and feeling more like himself.

"Yeah, I've known Rob for several years, ever since I opened up my shop here. He's become a great and supportive friend."

Just then, Rob and Ben approached them.

"Can we get a photo together, guys?" Rob asked.

The photographer captured a few posed and candid shots, and Neil asked to see Ben's ring.

"Matthew, you'll need to tell me more about the materials you used. The rings are gorgeous."

"I promise I will." He smiled. "But if you'll excuse me, I want to say hello to Judge Sampson."

As he departed, Jon turned to Neil. "Are you okay, dude? You looked like a deer in the headlights for a minute there."

"I'm fine now, I think. Matthew seems like a really great guy. I think I want to get to know him better."

"Well, you'll get your chance," Jon said with a knowing smile. "He'll be on the cruise with us."

CHAPTER 3

Friday, October 7, Westport, Massachusetts—Later That Day

Matthew cornered Sam in the kitchen.

"So what's the deal with Neil?" He tried to sound nonchalant but wasn't sure he succeeded.

"Oh, Kyle's friend?" Sam said coyly. "He and Kyle work together. He's a good guy. And to answer the questions that are obviously spinning around in that pretty little head of yours,"—the sides of Sam's mouth quirked into a smile—"he's twenty-nine, gay, and single."

"Um, that's not really what I meant," Matthew stammered. "I, um, I just hadn't really heard about him before. Besides, it's not like I'd have a chance with someone like him." He felt warmth rise to his cheeks. He was thankful that his dark skin would hide most of the blush that was surely there.

"Don't sell yourself short, Matthew. You've several years older than him, but I don't think that makes a damn bit of difference. After all, look at Kyle and Jon. By the way, Neil will be on the cruise too. Maybe you can get to know him a little better on the ship."

"Oh, good to know. Well, I'm gonna head back outside. There are a few folks I haven't said hello to yet." He made a hasty retreat out onto the deck, trying not to think of Sam standing there with a huge smile on her face.

———

By a little after three o'clock, the caterers, photographer, DJ, and most of the guests had left.

Those remaining in the house would be leaving for Boston's Logan Airport at four for their flight to Barcelona. A few folks who had been invited weren't able to attend, but Rob and Ben would be joined by Kyle and Jon, Sam, Ben's assistant, Julie, Mike and Ellen, Mike Jr., Becky and Wyatt, Neil, and Matthew.

They'd all brought their luggage to the house with them earlier and were now using bathrooms and spare bedrooms to change.

Matthew joined the others in the family room, now wearing dark jeans and a maroon Henley.

"Can I get you something to drink while we wait, Matthew?" Ben asked.

Looking around the room, Matthew saw several folks with glasses, so he said, "Sure, some red wine would be great, thanks."

He sat in an overstuffed chair next to the sofa, and Ben handed him a glass of wine.

"We're really glad you decided to join us on the cruise."

"Thanks, Ben. I still think it's too much, but Christine and Sam both convinced me that I need to do this. They reminded me that I haven't had a real vacation in several years, so this will do me good. And it's off-season, so Christine can certainly handle everything while I'm gone."

"I'm glad they talked you into it. It's important to take care of yourself, and Rob and I are thrilled that we can help you do that."

"In fact," Rob said, moving next to Ben and addressing the room, "we're so happy that all of you are able to join us on the cruise. Each and every one of you are important to us, and this is our way of saying 'thank you' for being part of our lives."

They chatted amicably about the trip. Matthew admitted he'd never been on a cruise before, and Jon and Neil told everyone they hadn't either.

"Well," Jon admitted, "I did do that river cruise with Kyle this summer, but he assures me this will be nothing like that." Kyle promised to help all the new cruisers, and Rob voiced his support as well.

Just before four o'clock, the doorbell rang, and a few moments later Rob announced that the driver had arrived to transport them to Boston. People and luggage loaded, they sat back and continued to chat about the cruise during their hour-plus ride to Logan Airport.

There were only twelve adults, plus Wyatt, who sat on his dad's lap, but Rob and Ben had hired a van that could hold more than twenty, so they were able to spread out a bit. Neil was seated toward the back of the vehicle, and when Matthew got on, he sat behind him.

"Are you nervous about the cruise at all?" he asked Neil in an attempt to begin a conversation.

"Not really. Sure, the idea of being surrounded by water, on a ship made of steel, that my mind is trying hard to tell me shouldn't possibly float, had me concerned a bit, but Kyle managed to convince me that it's perfectly safe."

Matthew laughed. "Wow, that's certainly convincing."

"I, um, well, I didn't mean it like that," Neil sputtered.

"I'm only teasing you," Matthew said, not quite believing that he was actually flirting pretty shamelessly. He never did such things. "Actually, I pretty much felt the same way. But both Rob and Ben explained that it really is perfectly safe, and that I deserve to take some time to pamper myself, so here I am."

"Well, I think that since we're both 'cruise virgins,' as it were, we should probably stick together and work through our fears."

"That's a wonderful idea," agreed Matthew. He reached out his hand to shake Neil's hand and seal their pact.

As they shook, Matthew's hand tingled. Something electrical seemed to pass through him, and his heart beat just a bit faster. *What the hell was that? Did Neil feel it too?*

"We will be fine and have a fantastic time," Neil reiterated.

"I still can't believe that Rob and Ben are taking us all on this cruise with them," Matthew said. It was a poor attempt at continuing the conversation, but he desperately wanted to chat more even though he was usually awkward in situations when he met new people socially. "And I guess I'm particularly surprised that they invited me."

"I know what you mean," Neil said. "Kyle explained it all to me when I got my invitation, but it still feels like it's too much. But Rob and Ben are both very generous, and I finally agreed that I owed it to myself. Like you said, a bit of pampering is a good thing, right?"

"It really is. My assistant at the shop reminded me that I hadn't taken a vacation in too long and practically helped me pack my bags." Matthew chuckled. "But she's right. I tend to bury myself in work and never really do anything for myself."

"Wow, your assistant sounds like Kyle. He told me that I needed to, quote, 'Get my ass on that ship and enjoy myself for a change.' I guess we're lucky that we have friends that care about us so much."

"Yes, we are. So now that we've decided to heed their advice, what are you looking forward to doing on the cruise? Since we're in the virgin cruisers club together, we need to discuss these things."

Their conversation turned to all things cruise related, and the trip to the airport passed quickly.

At Rob and Ben's request, Sam had booked everyone in business class, so check-in was quick, and the lines at security weren't too bad. Before they knew it, Rob was herding everyone toward the airline's club lounge, where they could relax and wait for their flight.

There wasn't a large number of seats available together, so folks spread out a bit. Matthew saw Neil sitting with Kyle and Jon off to one side of the lounge. As he was scanning the space for a spot to sit, Sam caught his eye. She and a woman named Julie were sitting at the bar, and there was one more seat available.

"Matthew," Sam called. "Come sit with us."

"Thanks," he said, dropping down on the available barstool.

"Matthew, this is Julie Samuelson, Ben's assistant. Julie, this is Matthew Palmer, jewelry designer extraordinaire."

"Pleased to meet you, Julie," Matthew said, shaking her outstretched hand.

"Likewise, Matthew," Julie replied. "And I'm more like just Ben's friend now. Since he's pretty much retired from acting, I don't really do much of anything for him anymore.

"And Matthew," Julie continued, "your designs are gorgeous. I was in England with everyone when Rob gave Ben the bracelet for Christmas, and I saw the rings earlier. You're extremely talented."

"Thank you." Matthew blushed.

The bartender came over to them, and after they'd ordered drinks, Matthew said, "I know you've cruised before, Sam, but what about you, Julie?"

"Once with my family," Julie replied. She was a petite woman, with very short dark hair, flawless dark-copper skin, and a wide smile. Her deep, chocolate-brown eyes sparkled behind bright, purple-framed glasses. "It was a short Caribbean cruise from Florida, and I enjoyed it, but I'm really looking forward to this one."

"This is all so new to me," Matthew said. "I never expected my first cruise to be in the Mediterranean. Oh, who am I kidding, I never expected to take a cruise at all."

The bartender returned with their drinks, and after a quick toast to a fun vacation, Matthew continued, "So, what's the first thing I need to know about the cruise before we get to the ship?"

"Try to relax, and don't expect to be able to do everything," Sam replied. "I know that Rob and Ben have a few things planned—don't worry, you'll find out more once we're all on board—but you'll have plenty of time to do some things on your own if you want. Just enjoy yourself. That's what this is all about."

Julie nodded in agreement. "Yeah, I don't think any of us really relax enough in our day-to-day lives, so this is a good time to just spend some time doing what you enjoy but never have time for at home. I'm planning on signing up for some spa treatments; I'm definitely getting a massage and facial and probably a manicure and pedicure too."

"Oh, a massage sounds like a great idea," Matthew said. "I did watch a few videos about the ship and saw the spa area. I thought I'd look into that since the thermal pool and sauna sounded like something interesting to try."

"They have a package for the entire cruise," Sam said. "I'm thinking of signing up for that, and I'm pretty sure some of the others will be interested. When I cruised with Rob a couple of years ago, we went to the spa every morning and spent an hour switching between the pool, sauna, and steam room. It's one of my favorite things to do on a day at sea."

"Sounds good to me," Matthew said, lifting his glass to sip the bourbon he'd ordered. "I was chatting with Neil earlier, and since he and I are both cruise virgins, we agreed to stick together and help each other get through the whole cruise experience. I'll mention the spa stuff to him and see if he's interested."

"I think that's a wonderful idea," Sam effused. "It's always fun to see first-time cruisers experience all the ship has to offer. I'm looking forward to seeing what you and Neil think of it all."

Matthew found the business-class section of the aircraft interesting. He'd flown a few times but never to Europe, and business class was also a new experience for him. The seats were almost podlike, and they were arranged in pairs, with one seat facing forward and the other facing toward the back of the plane.

After pulling his Kindle out of his backpack and storing the pack in the overhead compartment, he sat down and found himself facing Neil in the other seat.

"Wow, I've never done anything like this before," Matthew said in awe. "This is amazing."

"Yeah, it is," Neil agreed. "I've only flown in business class once before with Kyle. I never thought it would happen again, but hey, I'm not complaining. The food is better than what you get in coach, and the drinks are free."

"That's cool, but I'm not sure how much I'll get to enjoy it. I'm pretty sure I'll fall asleep at some point."

"I usually nap a bit on these overnight flights," Neil said. "They'll probably serve dinner and drinks shortly after we take off, and then we'll have time to doze for a while. And then there'll be breakfast before we land in London. There should be a menu in the pocket next to the flat screen."

A flight attendant walked by and offered them a flute of champagne before takeoff, and they both accepted.

"Cheers," Neil said with a smile. "Here's to a great vacation."

As Neil had predicted, once airborne, drink and food orders were taken. Matthew was pleased that they had Woodford Reserve bourbon and ordered some on the rocks. They chatted amicably during dinner, then both read for a while. Soon Matthew felt his eyes getting heavy, and he stowed his e-reader.

Lowering his seat into a lie-flat position, he said, "I'm finding it hard to keep my eyes open. I'm going to try and sleep for a bit."

"Sweet dreams," Neil replied. "I'm probably going to do the same."

CHAPTER 4

After a brief layover in London and a short flight to Barcelona, the group was met outside of baggage claim by a tall woman with short dark hair holding a sign that read ASHER-ROCKINGHAM PARTY.

"*Buenos días, soy el señor Rock—um, Asher-Rockingham,*" Ben said as he approached the woman.

Neil was standing to Ben's right, and he noticed him stumble a bit over his new last name. He smiled, thinking it would take a while for both of them to get used to that.

"*Buenos días. Soy Carmella. Sígueme, por favor,*" she replied.

They all followed her a short distance to a large van with storage in the back for their bags. Once everything was stored and they were all seated, Carmella turned to Ben, who was sitting in the front seat. "Just to confirm, you are going to the Hotel L17 on Rambla Catalunya, correct?"

"Yes," Ben replied.

"If traffic is not bad, we should be there in less than an hour."

Never having been to Barcelona before, Neil, along with several of the others, spent the trip looking out the windows and enjoying the scenery.

Before long, they arrived at their hotel and proceeded to the lobby.

"Ben and Sam will take care of getting us all checked in," Rob announced to the group. "Leave your luggage here for now, and we can head into the bar so that we don't take up all the space in the lobby."

After placing their bags along the wall near one of the reception desks, they all followed Rob down a short hall to the bar.

A gentleman standing behind the bar looked up when they entered and smiled widely. "Señor Asher, so good to see you again!"

He moved out from behind the bar and hugged Rob.

"Good to see you too, Carlos," Rob replied. "And it's Asher-Rockingham now."

"*¡Felicitaciones!*"

"*Gracias*," replied Rob. He gestured to the group surrounding him.

"This is our family," he said. "They're joining us on a cruise tomorrow to celebrate. Ben and Samantha are getting us checked in, but perhaps we could have some prosecco while we're waiting?"

"Of course, my friend."

Some sat at the bar while others stood, and they all chatted animatedly.

"I still can't believe I'm actually here with you all," Neil said to Kyle and Jon. "I keep expecting to wake up and find this has all been a dream."

"Oh, it's real," said Kyle. "Wait until you get on the ship. It's only gonna get better."

A few minutes later, Ben and Sam arrived and were handed glasses of sparkling wine.

"Okay," Ben started, "everyone is checked in, and Sam has all the key cards. The rooms will be ready in about fifteen minutes, so relax and have another glass of prosecco if you'd like. Once we know everything is all set, Sam will pass out the keys, and you can head upstairs."

He glanced at his watch. "It's almost lunchtime, so if you want to grab a bite to eat, there are some great places nearby. See me or Rob or Sam, and we'll let you know what's available. If you didn't sleep much on the plane and want to crash, that's fine too." Several of them chuckled.

"And whatever you do, please be back down here in the lobby by seven thirty. Rob and I have made reservations at a wonderful seafood restaurant nearby. Carmella will be back with the van to take us there."

"Jon and I are planning on getting some tapas for lunch," Kyle said to Neil. "Do you want to join us?"

"Sure. I managed to sleep for a few hours, and frankly, I'm just a bit too excited to sleep more at this point."

He glanced over and saw Matthew talking with Julie and Sam.

"Is it okay if I ask them if they'd like to join us?" He pointed at the three of them.

"Sure. The more the merrier."

Neil ambled over to the small group. "Kyle, Jon, and I are

going to get some tapas for lunch in a little while. Would any of you like to join us?"

"Thanks, but I didn't sleep as well as I'd hoped on the flight," Matthew said. "I think I'm just going to crash for a bit."

"I've been telling Julie about this great shop not far from here, so we're going shopping," Sam said excitedly. "But let me know where you're going, and maybe we'll stop by after we're done with our retail therapy."

"Okay, I'll ask Kyle and let you know," said Neil.

Just then, a member of the hotel staff approached Sam to say the rooms were ready for everyone.

"Dad said this place is just a few blocks down on the left," Kyle said as they headed down the street. "Apparently, this is the place they had dinner together the night they met."

"I think it's so cool that they get to relive their meeting from two years ago," said Neil.

"Yeah," agreed Jon. "And the fact that we get to be with them is a bonus."

They reached the tapas restaurant that Ben had told them about. It wasn't busy, and they were able to snag a large table near the front window. That would give them extra room if Sam and Julie joined them later.

After ordering a pitcher of red sangria and a few small plates from the menu, Jon looked at Neil and said, "What do you think of Matthew so far?"

"I, um ... he seems nice, I guess. Why? What do you mean, Jon? I, um ... I just met him yesterday," Neil stammered.

"If I'm not mistaken, you called him, and I quote, 'a great guy' at the wedding. Plus, you kinda had one of those 'deer in the headlights' looks when you said it," Kyle added, smiling. "Jon and I talked about it on the flight, and we think you should go for it."

"What do you mean, 'go for it'?" Neil asked, a bit shocked.

"You know, get to know him better, ask him out for drinks or something on the cruise. Maybe even hook up," Jon said, grinning.

"No pressure, Neil," Kyle started, "but he's hot, single, and gay. Why not?"

"Yeah, he is hot," Neil agreed, blushing. "Do you know how old he is, by any chance?"

"He's thirty-seven," Kyle said. "Not that age should make a difference, right? Look at Jon and me."

"Not an issue at all," Neil agreed. "And Matthew looks younger. As you know, I've usually dated guys younger than me. Maybe that's been my problem all along."

"Yeah." Kyle looked at Jon and smiled. "Older guys are really the way to go."

"TMI but good to know. And yeah, so far Matthew's been really nice, and we've chatted a bit, but why would he want to spend time with someone like me? Kyle, you know I never have any luck with guys."

"Hey, don't put yourself down like that. Sure, you seem to have rotten taste in the men that you try to date, but maybe your luck is changing. I think you need to give this a try. Matthew certainly seemed interested when you guys were talking yesterday. And I know for a fact that he *is* a great guy."

"Okay," said Neil, sighing. "But no pressure, please, guys. I promise we'll spend time together, and if something happens, that's great. And if nothing happens, that's fine too."

"Fair enough," Kyle replied. "I really think you've got a chance here, my friend."

LUNCH WITH KYLE and Jon had been great but longer than Neil was used to. Sam and Julie had shown up as they were finishing, so that meant more sangria and conversation. He still managed to take a forty-minute power nap when he got back to his room. The wine consumed at lunch made it easy to fall asleep quickly.

After a quick washup, he felt refreshed and was more than ready for dinner with the gang.

Stepping off the elevator, Neil saw most of them were mingling in the lobby. Jon and Kyle were talking with Mike Jr. and Becky, so he headed in that direction.

"Hi, everyone." Turning to Becky, he said, "Where's that handsome son of yours?"

"Mom and Dad decided to skip the group dinner, so they offered to watch Wyatt for us," Becky replied.

"Is everything okay?" Neil asked.

"Oh yeah," answered Mike Jr. "Mom doesn't travel as well as she used to and tires more easily, so they decided to get a quick bite nearby and then make it an early night."

Rob walked in the hotel main doors and announced that Carmella was there, so they all went out to board the van.

DINNER WAS QUITE ENJOYABLE. Neil found himself seated beside Matthew and across from Kyle and Jon, and they chatted about all sorts of things over a delicious dinner of fresh seafood.

"Dad," Kyle began, "where was that place that you and Rob went to this summer? You never did finish telling us about it."

"It's a little town called Hawthorne Bluff," replied Ben. "It's on the coast of Massachusetts, just south of Plymouth. It's a beautiful little place. I think you and Jon should plan a getaway there."

"Oh, I've heard of it," Matthew said. "Never actually been there, but one of my customers mentioned it in the store one day not too long ago."

"It really is charming," Rob added, joining the conversation. "Sam recommended it to Ben a couple of months ago, when I was driving them both crazy with my wedding plans. It was either take me away for a couple of days or bury me in the backyard."

"Sam didn't want to break a nail digging a hole, so I took him on a romantic getaway," Ben chuckled, finishing the story.

Neil could feel the love emanating from Ben and Rob and hoped that he too would find that someday.

"Maybe we should plan a trip for next spring," Kyle said to Jon. "We can visit Dad and Rob for a few days and also spend some time there."

"Let me know if you decide on dates for that," Sam joined in. "I can see about making a reservation at the bed-and-breakfast for you."

As they finished their dessert of fresh fruit macerated in

prosecco, Ben stood and cleared his throat to get everyone's attention.

"I just wanted to take a moment and thank you all again for joining us for this continuing celebration. It means a lot to Rob and me that you're all here with us."

"We should be thanking you, Uncle Ben," Mike Jr. said. "This is the trip of a lifetime for us."

Neil heard murmurs of agreement around the table.

"Breakfast is from seven until ten tomorrow morning," Ben continued. "Carmella or someone else from the transportation company will be picking us up at ten thirty. It's a short ride to the pier, and we have a check-in time of eleven o'clock, so please be in the lobby and ready to go around ten fifteen. And remember to wear your OceanAccess wristband. It will help speed up the check-in process."

Rob had been settling up the bill with one of the waiters, and when he returned to the table, they all stood and went outside to the waiting van.

CHAPTER 5

Matthew woke to unfamiliar surroundings as the alarm on his phone sounded.

Barcelona. I'm in a hotel in Barcelona.

He padded into the bathroom and peed, then peered at his reflection in the mirror. He could go another day without shaving, he decided. After a quick shower, he brushed his teeth and dressed in black jeans and a short-sleeved, plum-hued Henley.

Once downstairs, he headed over to the restaurant and saw Kyle, Jon, and Neil sitting at a table near the windows. Jon waved him over.

"Good morning, guys," he said warmly. "How did everyone sleep?"

"I slept really well," Neil replied. "It usually takes me a night or two to get used to a new place, but I think all that wine with dinner last night helped."

They all chuckled. "Jon and I slept very well too," Kyle said. "And yes, the wine definitely helped. How about you, Matthew?"

"I was out as soon as my head hit the pillow," he answered. "I don't remember a thing until my alarm went off this morning."

"Coffee?" Jon asked as he picked up the carafe on the table.

"Yes, please," answered Matthew.

"There's a buffet set up over there." Neil pointed to an alcove in the rear of the space.

"Thanks. Can I get anyone anything?"

"I'll go with you," Kyle said. "There's another Danish calling to me, I think."

"Can you get me one too, sweetheart?" Jon asked.

"Sure. Anything for you, Neil?"

"No, I'm good, thanks."

Upon their return, conversation turned to the cruise and things they were hoping to do. A few minutes later, Rob and Ben walked into the restaurant, and after a brief greeting, went off to the buffet. The rest of their group arrived soon after, and before long, they were all enjoying breakfast and chatting excitedly among their tables.

"The van will be here in about fifteen minutes," Sam announced to the group. "If you can go up to your rooms and grab your luggage, that would be great. I'll be in the lobby to collect everyone's key cards, and I'll take care of checking everyone out of their rooms."

MATTHEW COULD FEEL the excitement in the van as they traveled the short distance to the cruise terminal.

"I still can't believe this is happening," Neil said to no one in particular. His face was quite animated, and Matthew caught himself staring.

God, he's beautiful. Those wide shoulders and that narrow waist, that dark hair and those piercing blue eyes; it's like he was made just for me.

"I know exactly what you mean," agreed Matthew. "I know I'll wake up from this dream at some point, but for now I'm going to enjoy every minute of it!"

Rob and Ben gave them all a rundown of what to expect at the pier and advised them all to stick together.

"Once we're on board, we should proceed to our muster stations to check in," Rob told everyone. "Even though our staterooms are all close together, we may have different muster locations, but we'll figure that out once we're on board."

"We can then all head to our cabins to drop off our carry-on bags," Ben added. "Rob and I would like you all to join us for a 'welcome aboard' drink. There's a bar called the Trident Lounge on Deck 8 in the area known as Seaside Cove."

"Once we've all had time to freshen up in our rooms, we'll send out a group text telling you what time to meet us there," Rob continued. "And don't forget, all the deck plans are in the OceanCruise app. You can also find a deck plan of the floor you're on near every elevator."

Ben looked around the van at everyone and smiled. "It might seem a bit overwhelming for you if you've not been on a cruise before, but it will get easier. Rob, Sam, and I are pretty familiar with the layout of the ship, so don't be afraid to reach out to us with any questions."

Their driver pulled into the pier facility, and everyone stared out the windows at the magnificent—and huge—ship before them.

"Oh my god," exclaimed Matthew. "It's gigantic!"

As Carmella parked the van near the entrance to the terminal building, Rob said, "All right, people, let this adventure begin!"

CHECK-IN WENT SMOOTHLY, and before he knew it, Matthew was walking with the rest of the group onto the ship. His head swiveled back and forth, his mouth agape in disbelief as he tried to take in the wide concourse dotted with shops, restaurants, and bars.

"Pretty impressive, isn't it?" Rob said from behind him. "This is the Ocean Promenade, and it runs the length of the ship from the bank of forward elevators to the ones at the aft."

"It's hard to believe this is a cruise ship," Matthew admitted. "It feels more like I'm at a mall or something."

"I agree, but wait until you see Seaside Cove." Rob winked at him, smiling broadly. "It's really gonna blow you away."

"I checked, and it seems we're divided between two different muster stations," Sam addressed their small group. "Follow me, everyone. We're going to head down to the Coral Reef Lounge." She pointed toward the aft end of the ship. "If you have a C3 notation in the OceanAccess app, you'll check in at the Coral Reef. If you have a C2, check in across the way at the Seven Seas Pizzeria. Look for the crew with the neon-green vests and hats. Once you're done with that, take an elevator up to Deck 12 and find your stateroom."

"I'll send out a group text in about ten minutes letting you know what time to meet in the Trident Lounge on Deck 8," Ben added.

They all managed to check in at their muster stations in record time and rode two elevators up to Deck 12.

"Our staterooms are all together along the back of the ship, with Neil and Matthew's cabins curving around to the starboard side," Rob said. "And remember, since they're all suites, we have a dedicated pair of Ocean Navigators who can take care of reservations and such for us during the cruise. Think of them as butlers or valets on steroids—if there's anything you need, reach out to them via telephone or the NavigatorChat in the app."

As they approached Matthew's cabin, which was the first in the group, Ben added, "Since we're all together here, I think we can skip the group text for now. Let's meet in the Trident Lounge on Deck 8 in about fifteen minutes. If you're afraid you'll get lost, meet us at our cabin, which is 12720, in ten minutes."

MATTHEW SHUT the suite door behind him and stared at what would be his accommodations for the next twelve days.

It was stunning!

But this has got to be a mistake. I know Rob and Ben said it was a suite, but I didn't expect something this large and opulent.

Standing in the small foyer, he dropped his backpack on the floor and gazed to the left, where he saw a bar area, complete with a coffee maker and shelves containing assorted glassware. A large bowl of fruit and a covered dish completed the scene. In front of the bar was a spacious living room with deep-green carpeting and furniture upholstered in various shades of blue and green. A couple of tangerine-and-yellow patterned pillows added a pop of color to the sofa and chairs.

The far wall was all windows, and as he moved closer, he realized there were sliding glass doors leading to a large balcony. On the right, an archway led into an enormous bedroom with a king-sized bed, all done in tranquil shades of cream and seafoam green. Along one wall were several doors, which turned out to be closets.

Matthew had noticed another door on the right when he'd entered the suite, so he went back and opened it, only to find a marbled bathroom, complete with whirlpool tub, separate shower, double vanity, toilet, and bidet.

He shook his head, in awe at everything.

"What did I do to deserve friends like this?" he wondered silently.

He heard a faint tapping and walked back into the living room. Neil was standing on his balcony, knocking on his sliding door.

"Hey, Neil," he said, opening the slider.

"Hey. So we're neighbors, and the partition between our balconies is open, so I thought I'd come over and say hi. Is this fucking incredible or what? Oh, um, sorry," he stammered, "I didn't mean to curse."

"It's fine," Matthew agreed, "and 'fucking incredible' sums it up nicely. Come on in."

"I can't believe these suites," Neil said. "Looks like we have matching rooms. Mine's a mirror image."

"If we have rooms like this, I can't even imagine what the rest of them are like."

"Right? But I'm sure we'll see them soon enough," Neil agreed.

Just then, they heard something out on the balcony and saw Jon and Kyle walking around the corner onto Neil's veranda.

"Hey, guys," Kyle said as they moved back onto the balcony. "Isn't this great?"

"I called it fucking incredible, and Matthew agreed with me." Neil laughed, and the others joined in. "What's your suite like?"

"Come see. The balconies are all opened up to each other, so we can move around. Our bedroom is a loft!" Jon was visibly excited and could barely get the words out.

When they reached Kyle and Jon's balcony, Matthew once again stopped and stared. Their veranda wrapped around the corner of the ship and was immense.

Inside was a large living room with a separate dining area, holding a table that could seat six people. A curved staircase led up to the loft, which had a large bedroom that overlooked the living area, a spacious bathroom with a double shower, and a second, smaller balcony that looked out over the side of the ship.

"Incredible," Matthew uttered. "I never dreamed that there were cabins like this on a cruise ship."

"Cruise lines have really gone all out in the past few years," Kyle said. "Cabins on older ships aren't this fancy, but the newer ships are all trying to outdo each other with suites like this. If I'm not mistaken, my dad and Rob have a suite like this, and the three in between us are similar but maybe just a tad smaller."

Jon glanced at his watch. "I don't want to break up this party, but we should probably head down to Seaside Cove."

THEY PASSED through the automatic doors on Deck 8 leading to Seaside Cove.

Matthew found himself once again staring at the scene before him, mouth agape.

"I felt exactly the same way, Matthew," said Ben, standing beside him chuckling. "It doesn't seem possible for this to be on a ship, does it?"

"It's unbelievable!" Matthew exclaimed.

There was a stone pathway winding through the area, with islands of plants throughout. Palm trees swayed in the open air, with ficus and other trees and bushes rounding out the display. Hibiscus and other flowering plants were interspersed with the greenery, and an occasional water fountain could be seen.

On either side of the cove were restaurants and bars and the occasional specialty shop.

"There are somewhere between twelve and fourteen thousand live plants here," Ben said as they meandered along. "And they have a team of four arborists to maintain the area."

"Oh my god, is that a koi pond?" Matthew asked, pointing to a small aquatic feature they passed.

"Yeah," replied Rob. "And above those restaurants and shops are balcony cabins that overlook the entire area."

Matthew turned to the right and saw that they'd reached

the Trident Lounge. A large bar ran the length of the venue, and there was seating both inside and out. The outdoor area looked like it was a sandy beach, with round tables featuring colorful umbrellas. They grabbed a couple of large tables close to the far end of the bar.

A few moments later, a bar waiter approached the tables.

"Welcome to the Trident Lounge," he said. "I am Sergey. May I get you something to drink?"

After they'd placed their orders, they began chatting amongst themselves while they waited for their beverages to arrive.

"Pinch me, 'cause this can't be real," Neil said to Matthew.

"I know, right?" Matthew agreed, reaching over to lightly pinch Neil's leg.

At Neil's shocked expression, Matthew said, "Oh, I'm sorry! That was rather forward of me, wasn't it? It's just all the excitement of being on board, I'm sure." He felt himself blushing.

"Don't worry about it, Matthew," Neil reassured him. "I kind of asked for that, didn't I? Just didn't really expect anyone to take me up on it." He laughed good-naturedly, and Matthew felt himself relax. The last thing he wanted to do was offend this handsome man.

"Kyle was right. This is nothing like the river cruise he and I did earlier this year," Jon said. "I just know I'm going to get lost at some point."

"Actually, the app can give you directions, so that's less likely to happen," Kyle said. "I've not been on a ship this large, but I've found that after a couple of days, you start to recognize things on the ship, and it gets easier."

Sam joined in, "That's right, Kyle. And the next time you're near an elevator, check out the large monitor there. It knows where you are, and if you pick another spot on the ship, it will show you how to get there on the deck plan. I'm sure you'll all be fine."

Sergey arrived with their drinks, and they all helped pass them around.

Ben stood up and looked at each one of them. Raising his glass, he said, "Once again, thank you all so much for joining us on this cruise. We hope you have a fantastic time. Cheers!"

They toasted those around them and sipped their refreshments.

"Since tomorrow's a sea day," Sam said to those near her," does anyone have plans for what they'd like to do on the ship?"

Thus began an animated discussion of the ship's activities.

CHAPTER 6

Monday, October 10, at Sea

Standing in the shower, Neil thought about the conversation he'd had with Kyle and Jon in Barcelona. Yeah, okay, he was attracted to Matthew a little. Well, maybe more than a little.

Matthew was quite handsome, and his entire face lit up when he smiled. Neil usually dated guys that were several inches shorter than him, but when they stood together, he and Matthew were almost eye to eye, and there was something really nice about that.

Of course, they weren't dating, but Neil wanted to get to know Matthew better. Perhaps it would just turn into a friendship and nothing else, but that was okay too. And if it developed into something more, well, Neil wouldn't say no to that at all.

He thought about what he wanted to do today while he dressed. He chose a cobalt-blue polo to pair with jeans and sneakers. For all the talking they had done yesterday over drinks and then later at dinner, he thought he might just want to take it easy on the first day.

But first things first, he needed breakfast—especially coffee—to start the day. Grabbing his phone and Kindle, he went in search of the Bluefin Bistro, the restaurant exclusively for passengers staying in suites on the ship. It was the same spot where they'd had dinner last night, so he was pretty sure he could find it again. After he ate, he'd play it by ear. Perhaps walk around the ship a bit and get to know where a few things were located, then find a quiet spot to read for a while.

As he approached the hostess at the doorway to the bistro, she looked up at him and said, "Good morning, sir. Are you dining alone this morning?"

"Yes, plea—" He paused, catching a glimpse of Matthew sitting alone at a table near the window. "Excuse me," he said. "That gentleman is part of the group I'm traveling with. Let me ask if I can join him."

"Certainly, sir."

He strode to the table, hoping he wasn't making a fool of himself by intruding on Matthew's breakfast.

"Good morning, Matthew. Would it be okay if I joined you? Um, that is, um, if you're not expecting anyone." *Dammit, I sound like an idiot. Don't be nervous. He's just a friend.*

"Oh, hi, Neil." Matthew sounded genuinely pleased to see him. "No, I'm not expecting anyone, and you can certainly join me if you'd like."

"Thanks." As Neil sat down, the hostess came over and handed him a menu.

"Enjoy your breakfast, gentlemen."

"Did you sleep okay?" Neil asked, trying to start a conversation and *not* sound like he was daft.

"Yeah, I did," Matthew replied. "I love the water and find the sound of it very soothing. I left the balcony door open when I was getting ready for bed last night, and that helped relax me after a very exciting day yesterday." He paused to sip his coffee. "What about you?"

"I did too, actually," Neil said. "That surprised me a bit since I often have trouble sleeping in a new place. Even though the seas are quite calm, I could feel a gentle rocking once I went to bed. I think that, combined with the alcohol we consumed at dinner, helped put me to sleep quicker than usual."

Matthew chuckled. "Yeah, I drank more than I normally do yesterday. I'm gonna need to behave myself on this trip."

A waiter approached carrying a carafe and asked Neil if he wanted coffee.

"Yes, please," he replied.

"Are you ready to order?" the waiter asked.

"I'd like the fresh fruit with yogurt," Matthew said. "And some wheat toast, please. Do you have any peanut butter?"

"Yes sir, we do. I'll bring some with your toast."

"A man after my own heart," Neil said with a laugh. "I love peanut butter. I'll have the same for breakfast, please."

"Certainly, sir. I'll be back shortly with your orders."

"It's so nice to find a fellow peanut-butter lover," Matthew said.

"I have a confession," Neil said, blushing a little. "I may

have packed some single-serve containers in my checked luggage. But I completely forgot to bring one with me this morning."

"That's hilarious." Matthew chuckled. "And I wish I had thought of it."

"Well, at least they have some on board. And if they happen to run out before the end of the cruise, I'll share my stash with you."

"Deal."

The waiter returned a few minutes later with their breakfast, refilled both coffee cups, and departed.

"Do you have any plans for today?" Neil asked as he smeared peanut butter onto one of the toast slices.

"I was thinking of walking around a bit and maybe figuring out where things are," Matthew answered. "I still can't believe we're on a cruise ship. I mean, everything is so large. It's nothing like I expected."

"I know exactly what you mean. I looked at some photos on the cruise line's website and watched a video, but it's still so much more than I expected."

Neil sipped his coffee and continued, "I was planning on exploring a bit too. Maybe we could check things out together? Might keep us from getting too lost."

"That's a great idea," Matthew effused. "I gotta admit, it seemed a bit overwhelming to try and discover things all on my own."

"If you remember correctly, before we left on this trip, we cruise virgins agreed to stick together." Neil smiled brightly. "We've got this."

The thought of spending at least part of the day with Matthew made everything seem a bit brighter.

AFTER SPENDING a few hours together roaming around the ship, they found themselves back at the Bluefin Bistro for a quick lunch.

"Whew," Neil uttered as he sat at their table. "That was fun!"

"It was, " Matthew agreed. "But it just confirms how amazingly huge this ship is. The app on my phone says we walked almost four miles this morning."

"I believe it. But since we're getting all this exercise, that just means we can eat more, right?" Neil asked innocently.

"Well, of course," Matthew said. "That's what vacation is all about."

They laughed, and Neil sighed. "Thanks for letting me join you this morning. It wouldn't have been nearly as much fun doing it alone."

"Of course. So what are you thinking of having for lunch?" Matthew asked.

"The Cobb salad, I think. Not too heavy, and despite what I said about eating more, I do need to watch my weight." Neil patted his belly self-consciously.

"Oh, please, from what I'm seeing, you've got nothing to worry about."

"Thanks," Neil said shyly.

"I think I'll have the Cobb too."

After they placed their lunch order, Matthew asked, "So, what's up for this afternoon? More exploring, or do you have something else in mind?"

"After all that exercise we managed to accomplish this morning, I was thinking about lying out on my balcony for a while," Neil said. "The weather is nice, and I thought I could read for a little while. Would you like to join me?"

They had plans to meet Kyle, Jon, Sam, and Julie for dinner at Kaiyo tonight. It was an Asian restaurant featuring a teppanyaki area where they cooked dinner at your table.

"That sounds great," Matthew said. "I'm anxious to get back into the book I'm currently reading. I was too tired last night to even try to read anything."

"Do you read a lot? Obviously I do since I don't go anywhere without my Kindle," Neil replied, tapping the cover of his e-reader on the table.

"I do, but I sometimes struggle to find something good to read. I forgot my Kindle in my cabin this morning—I blame the lack of caffeine before breakfast." Matthew laughed. "If you hadn't joined me for breakfast, I would have probably read on my phone."

"What do you like to read?" Matthew asked. "Maybe I can recommend a few things."

"Well, I like gay romance." Matthew blushed and lowered his eyes. "And I also like murder mysteries, especially if they have gay characters. I dunno, I just prefer characters that I can relate to more, but frankly, I'm willing to try just about anything."

"Oh, perfect!" Neil said. "I can recommend so many books to you. I love gay romance too, and mysteries—yes, please. You need to join our book-chat group."

"Um, you have a book-chat group? Tell me more," Matthew said, sounding excited.

"Yeah, we do," Neil said. "It's really informal. I think it started with Rob and Sam and Julie, then Jon and Kyle got added. And Ben finally caved and joined too since Rob was talking about it all the time. When Kyle mentioned it to me, I had him add me in too. We recommend books and authors to each other and occasionally talk about certain books we like or don't like. We've even done a FaceTime chat a few times when several of us wanna talk about a particular book."

"That sounds great," agreed Matthew. "So how do I join?"

"Gimme your cell number, and I'll add you in. I'll also send you a separate text so that you have my number. And I can send you a list of some of our favorite authors."

"Thanks so much," Matthew said, grinning widely.

Just then, the waiter arrived with their meals, and they dug in as they continued to chat about books.

———

WHEN THEY ARRIVED at their staterooms, they split up, agreeing to meet on Neil's balcony after they'd changed.

Neil opened the sliding doors leading to his balcony and double-checked to make sure the panel separating his balcony from Matthew's was still open. While there, he tossed his Kindle on one of the lounge chairs. Back in his suite, he quickly stripped and looked at the new bathing suits he'd bought for this trip. He typically preferred loose board shorts, but for the cruise he had purchased a couple of trunk-style suits, which were both briefer and tighter than what he usually wore.

He chose the navy-blue one that had a bright orange stripe down each side and slipped it on. Grabbing one of the beach towels from the closet, he headed toward the sliders and stopped short in his tracks.

Matthew was standing at the balcony railing, gazing out

to sea. He was wearing a bright-yellow bathing suit that hugged his ass perfectly.

Oh my god, Neil thought, *he's gorgeous.*

Matthew turned and smiled widely. Neil scanned his smooth, dark chest and forced himself not to stare at the considerable bulge in the front of Matthew's shorts.

"Hi, Matthew," he said somewhat awkwardly.

"It's such a beautiful day. I'm glad you suggested this," Matthew said, walking to the loungers. He picked up a tube of sunscreen and began applying it to his chest and arms.

"People think that just because I have a natural tan"—his eyes twinkled as he spoke—"that I don't need to wear sunscreen, but let me tell you, I can burn with the best of them, and it can be difficult to see, so I always slather this on."

Fuck, if I don't stop staring, I'm gonna come right here!

"Oh, I left mine in the bathroom. Let me go and get it," Neil said.

"You can use mine if you want," Matthew said, tossing the tube to Neil. He bent over and rubbed the lotion onto his legs.

"Thanks." Neil began applying the sunscreen to his body, discreetly catching glimpses of Matthew's glistening body.

"I'll grab a couple of bottles of water." Neil retreated into the cabin once he'd finished rubbing on the lotion. When he returned, Matthew was stretched out on one of the lounge chairs, Kindle in hand.

They read quietly for about thirty minutes, enjoying the sun and the light breeze.

Matthew put down his Kindle, and turning to Neil, said, "I need to turn over. Would you mind putting some lotion on my back?"

"Oh, sure, um, no problem," Neil replied, trying to think pure thoughts. "But then you'll need to do me too."

He paused, realized what he had said, and blushed. "Um, I mean put some on my back too."

Matthew laughed. "Sure, I can do that."

After taking care of each other, they lay on their stomachs and continued to read. A few minutes later, Neil heard a buzz and looked over to Matthew, who was reading something on his phone.

"Fuck," he said, looking at the screen. "Why did you have to tell him? Shit."

He stood quickly and stumbled to the balcony railing.

"Matthew? What's wrong?" Neil asked, wondering what had just happened.

"My brother Micah slipped up and told my dad that I was away on vacation with some friends." Matthew sighed.

"Okay," Neil said. "I don't mean to pry, but why is that a problem?"

"Well, um, Dad's response wasn't great," Matthew started. "See, he's not the most supportive guy. Huh. Yeah, that's an understatement. Dad's turned into quite the homophobe and said, 'It's not with *those* people, is it?'" He shook his head and stared out at the cerulean water. "I'm sorry, forget I said anything. We were having such a nice, peaceful time, and I had to go and ruin it."

"Don't be silly, you've got nothing to be sorry about," Neil said, standing by his side. "I'm sorry you have to deal with that shit. And I'm sorry that your dad doesn't see what a great guy you are." He slowly put his arm around Matthew's shoulders, trying to show his support.

"Thanks. I should be used to it by now, but every time

something like this happens, it just wears me down a little more. I'm sure he didn't mean to cause trouble, but I wish Micah hadn't said anything."

"It's okay. I'm here if you want to talk. About this or anything."

"I appreciate that, Neil. I don't talk about this stuff a lot, but I'll keep that in mind." He smiled weakly as if he were trying to shake off the bad feelings he was experiencing.

"I don't think I feel like reading anymore, but I would like a drink. I think I remember seeing a bottle of wine in the fridge; I'll be right back."

While he was gone, Neil picked up his phone and opened the Music app. He picked out a playlist of upbeat tunes, hoping to ease Matthew out of his funk.

CHAPTER 7

After a couple of glasses of wine, Matthew felt more relaxed. He and Neil had sat on the balcony, not really talking but just enjoying the scenery together. Neil had put some music on while he was grabbing the wine and two glasses; he knew Neil was trying to make him feel better, and he was touched by the gesture.

When the wine was gone, Matthew stood up. "I think I'm gonna take a nap before dinner. If I don't, I'll probably fall asleep in my miso soup."

Neil rose as well. "A nap sounds really good at this point," he agreed. "But if you need anything, please call me."

"Thanks, I appreciate that."

They hugged, and Matthew was a bit surprised that it didn't feel awkward at all. He hadn't known Neil for long, but he felt totally comfortable spending time with him.

Once back in his cabin, he stripped off his swim trunks

and took a quick shower to wash off the lotion. The cool water felt great against his skin, and as he stood there letting the water cascade over his shoulders and back, he felt himself relax even more.

Once dry, he set an alarm and drifted off to sleep thinking about how good it had felt when he hugged Neil.

AFTER SLEEPING for a couple of hours, Matthew felt refreshed. He still had time before dinner, so he thought he'd walk around a bit and stop somewhere for a drink. Perhaps he'd run into someone from the group.

Meandering along Deck 5, he passed the Coral Reef Lounge and spotted Rob and Ben sitting at the bar. He debated whether or not to approach them, but Ben chose that moment to turn and do some people watching. Spotting Matthew, he waved and gestured for him to join them.

"Hi, guys," Matthew said cheerfully when he reached them. "What's going on?"

"Not much," replied Rob. "Would you like to join us for a drink?"

"Only if I'm not interrupting," he said sheepishly. "This is your honeymoon, after all."

"True," Ben said, chuckling. "But we did invite you along now, didn't we?"

"It's really more of a party than anything else," Rob added, smiling. "We wanted you and the others with us to celebrate and have fun. Now sit down and have a drink."

"Yes, sir," Matthew said as he sat in the free chair next to Rob. Turning to Ben, he asked, "Is he always this bossy?"

"Oh, you have no idea!"

"Hey, not fair, husband," Rob said, laughing.

A bartender approached, and Matthew ordered a glass of sauvignon blanc.

"What have you been up to on your first day, Matthew?" Ben asked.

"Not too much." The waiter placed the wine in front of him, and Matthew sipped before continuing.

"I saw Neil at breakfast, so we did a little bit of exploring this morning, just trying to get our bearings on the ship. There's just so much to see. Then after lunch, Neil and I hung out on his balcony and read for a bit."

Matthew paused, trying to decide if he should tell them about his brother's text.

"Is everything okay?" Rob asked.

"Yeah, why?" Matthew stared at him.

"I dunno. You just seemed serious all of a sudden."

"Well, while we were on the balcony, I got a text from Micah. It seems he told my dad I was on this cruise, and Dad may have made a negative remark or two."

"Ah, shit. Sorry about that," Ben said. Since Rob and Matthew had been friends for several years, he was aware of Matthew's family issues, and once Ben became part of Rob's family, he too was privy to Matthew's plight.

"It's not like I shouldn't be used to it by now." Matthew sighed. "Mom's a little better, but I can't see Dad changing at this point."

"It still sucks, and we're sorry you have to go through that," Rob added. "Did you say something to Neil? He didn't say or do anything to upset you, did he?"

"No, not at all," Matthew said. "I did tell him what

happened, and he was really nice; quite sweet about it, actually."

He paused, lifting the glass of wine to his lips. He debated asking them more about Neil since there seemed to be some attraction there.

"So," Matthew began, tentatively, "what can you tell me about Neil?"

He noticed a look pass between Rob and Ben but wasn't exactly sure what it meant.

"He's a really nice guy," Ben started. "Neil has been Kyle's best friend for years now, ever since they started working at the investment company. I know he's single, and from what little Kyle has said about it, he doesn't seem to have had much luck dating recently."

Matthew nodded thoughtfully.

"Why? Is there something more you want to know?" Ben asked. "You could probably talk to Kyle."

"No, nothing specific. I guess I just wanted to be sure you thought he was an okay guy."

"Oh?" Rob said. "Are you interested in him, Matthew?"

"I, um, well," Matthew started, feeling a bit flustered. "He is attractive. And I got the feeling he might be interested in me too. But I didn't want to start anything or get my hopes up if I was just imagining it."

He sighed again. "What am I even saying? It must be all in my head. Why would he be interested in someone like me?"

"Hey, none of that, now," Rob said gently. He put his arm around Matthew. "You're a handsome guy; you're fun and interesting. Why wouldn't Neil be interested?"

"Exactly," Ben agreed. "If you're interested in him, then I say go for it. Make plans to go on a shore excursion with him;

ask him to meet you for a drink. Get to know him a little better and see what happens."

"Okay, thanks, guys. I appreciate your talking to me about this. A group of us are doing an excursion to Rome tomorrow and Florence the day after, but we haven't planned anything for Naples yet. Maybe I'll talk to him about that."

"Sounds good to me," Rob said.

Dinner turned out to be a lot of fun. Sure, the chef told lots of corny jokes as he cooked their dinner on the flattop grill, but they all got to laugh and be silly together. Matthew couldn't remember the last time he felt so free and relaxed.

At one point during dessert, Sam announced that she and Julie were going to the dance club, called Change of Latitude, after dinner. They wanted to try and work off some of the day's calories on the dance floor. Kyle and Jon said they were heading back to their cabin, and the rest of the group looked at each other knowingly.

"I'm glad you have the energy to do that, Sam," Matthew said, "but I'm pretty much done in. Although feel free to dance for me." He winked at Sam and Julie. "I think I'm gonna stop somewhere for a nightcap and then head to bed."

"That actually sounds like a great idea," Neil agreed. "Do you mind if I join you, Matthew?"

"Not at all."

Leaving the restaurant, they walked along Seaside Cove and paused at the Trident Lounge. It wasn't overly busy, and there was a pianist off to the side playing some easy-listening melodies.

"How about here? Seems like a nice quiet ending to a great day."

"Perfect, Matthew."

They found a table for two in a rather secluded corner, and a waiter quickly approached to take their drink order.

"I know we already have plans for Rome tomorrow and Florence on Wednesday. But have you given any thought to what you want to do on Thursday in Naples, Neil?"

"Yes and no."

"Oh, well, that clears it up nicely." Matthew laughed.

"What I mean is, I heard Jon and Kyle talking about the shore trip to Pompeii, and I seriously thought about joining them for that, but frankly, after all the sightseeing we're doing over the next two days, I wanted something a bit more relaxing in Naples."

"That's exactly what I was thinking. I want to reserve some of my energy for Greece and Turkey."

"I was looking over the excursions available in Naples, and there's an easy walking tour in the morning. It's only about four hours long, and you get to see some of the architecture of the city. It ends with a lunch of a traditional Neapolitan pizza."

"That sounds great. You get to see some sights, but it's not too strenuous."

"Exactly. Would you like to join me for that, Matthew?"

"Yeah, I would, thanks. Can we book it on the app?"

"I'm pretty sure we can."

They pulled out their phones, and after a few minutes, they'd both booked the trip.

"And we'll still have a day and a half to relax before we

reach Mykonos." Matthew put his phone away, and after sipping his bourbon on the rocks, turned to Neil.

"I was chatting with Ben at one point, and he said that you really don't need to take a tour in Mykonos. It's a pretty small village that's easy to walk around, and he said to be sure to visit the windmills. I thought I'd just walk around for a bit and then grab lunch somewhere."

"Yeah, Sam said pretty much the same thing the other day. That'll be good as I'm sure we're in for a lot of exercise in Istanbul and Kusadasi."

They continued to chat about things to do and see in their upcoming ports, and before they knew it, their glasses were empty. Their waiter stopped by their table, but they both declined another drink.

They departed the lounge, heading toward the aft elevators, which were closest to their cabins.

As they reached the door to Matthew's suite, Neil stopped and looked at Matthew. Neil stared at him, not sure if he had the guts to do what he wanted. He'd been thinking about it all evening. *Okay, I'm gonna ask. He might say no, but I've got to go with my gut.*

"Would it be okay if I kissed you goodnight, Matthew?"

"Why, um, certainly."

Neil leaned in and kissed Matthew gently on the lips.

"I had a wonderful day with you today. Thank you for spending it with me."

"I enjoyed it too, Neil."

Neil pulled Matthew closer and kissed him again, running his right hand down Matthew's back while cradling his head with his left. *Ah, well, let's try this again.*

Opening his mouth ever so slightly, he ran his tongue

along the seam of Matthew's lips and felt him open his mouth slightly. Their tongues danced together, and Neil felt himself start to harden. He sucked gently on Matthew's tongue, then, not wanting to get too far ahead of himself, he ended the kiss and pulled away.

The slightly dazed look on Matthew's face told him that he'd enjoyed the kiss as much as Neil had.

"Sweet dreams, Neil. See you in the morning." Matthew smiled and opened the door to his stateroom.

Neil moved in for one more chaste kiss on the lips, whispered a sultry "good night," and moved down the hall to his own door.

***

OH MY GOD, that was so hot. And man, Neil is a great kisser!

Matthew closed the door behind him and tugged lightly at his stiffening cock.

It seems as if Neil is as interested in me as I am in him.

He undressed quickly and got into bed. He stroked his still hard dick and replayed the kiss in his mind. Before too long, he felt his balls tighten, and he thought again of that second kiss, when Neil sucked on his tongue. That was all it took; he shot hot cum all over his smooth belly.

Wow! It's been a while since I rubbed one out like that, but I definitely needed it after that kiss.

After cleaning himself up in the bathroom, he settled himself under the sheets and slowly drifted off to sleep.

Sweet dreams, indeed!

CHAPTER 8

There was no answer at Matthew's door, so Neil continued along the corridor to the elevators, lost in thought.

I'm really glad we kissed last night. That first one was nice, but that second kiss— god, that was hot!

He smiled, knowing he'd see Matthew soon and wondering what was in store for them.

Stepping off the elevator, he turned toward the Bluefin Bistro and saw Sam, Julie, and Matthew standing there chatting.

"Good morning, everyone." He placed his hand on Matthew's shoulder and gave it a slight squeeze as he greeted them.

"Are we ready to explore Rome today?"

"Yeah, but first I need coffee," Sam replied. Just then, Kyle and Jon arrived, and the hostess seated them for breakfast.

They quickly perused the menu and placed their orders. They were on a fairly tight schedule but had informed their waiter, so they shouldn't have any problems meeting their tour on time.

"I'm really looking forward to this," Jon said to no one in particular. "I've never been to Rome and want to see everything I can."

Julie beamed. "Me, too. From the description of the tour, it sounds like we'll hit the highlights. There are supposed to be stops at the Colosseum, the Spanish Steps, and the Trevi Fountain. Plus some general sightseeing from the bus. And then there's some free time for lunch and shopping."

"I was talking to Dad and Rob yesterday about today's tour," Kyle joined in. "Dad said there's a good chance the lunch stop will be at Campo de' Fiori—it's sort of a farmers-market area with several restaurants nearby. Rob gave me the names of a couple of places we might want to try for lunch."

"That sounds like a plan to me," Neil said, and they all nodded their agreement.

Just then their food arrived, and conversation dwindled as they hurried to eat before going to the theater to meet their tour group.

As they approached the Atlantis Theater, Sam announced to the group, "It's at least an hour into the city, more if we hit traffic. I'm sure there are facilities on the bus, but you may want to visit the restrooms before we leave."

"Yes, Mom," Kyle replied, smiling. But he and Jon both

veered off to the men's room, while Sam and Julie visited the ladies'.

"I limited my coffee intake this morning, so I should be okay for a while now," Neil said, shaking his head. "Um, sorry if that was TMI."

"No worries," Matthew laughed. "We all pee."

"Hey, not to change the subject; well, actually, I'm totally trying to change the subject ... do you want to sit together on the bus?"

"Yeah, that would be great," Matthew agreed.

The rest of their troupe returned, so they entered the theater together and waited for their group to be called.

THE TRIP to Rome was wonderful. They'd all managed to sit close together on the way into the city, chatting animatedly about what they would see in the city and admiring the scenery from the bus's large windows.

After several hours of sightseeing, they'd enjoyed a wonderful outdoor lunch at Campo de' Fiori. Neil had opted for the spaghetti carbonara, one of his favorite pasta dishes. A few went with salads and pizza, and Matthew chose a spicy pasta puttanesca. They ended up sharing most of the food along with a couple of bottles of wine and had a remarkable time.

By the time they boarded the bus for the ride back to the ship, they were pretty well beat. Matthew and Neil grabbed two seats together toward the back of the bus while the others found seats closer to the front.

"I think I'm going to end up snoozing on the ride back," Neil declared.

"Me, too. We walked quite a bit, and the wine at lunch kind of did me in," Matthew agreed.

They'd both worn light jackets when they had left the ship that morning, but it had warmed up a bit as the day progressed, so they ended up on their laps when they sat down.

Neil reached for Matthew's hand and slipped them both under the jackets between them, intertwining their fingers.

"Is this okay?" he asked quietly.

"Mmmm, more than okay."

As the bus exited the city, they both drifted off, Matthew's head resting on Neil's shoulder.

A while later, a bump in the road jostled them, and Neil woke. At first he was a bit disoriented but soon realized he was on the bus back to the ship. He was pleased to find he was still holding Matthew's hand. Glancing at the clock on his phone, he saw that it would still be a while before they arrived at the port in Civitavecchia. He wasn't sure if he'd sleep any more, but he stared out the window and reflected on the past twenty-four hours.

Matthew was definitely pushing all the right buttons. It had felt so comfortable hanging out with him yesterday; there weren't any awkward moments that he could remember. Even putting sunscreen on each other, which could have been weird since they hadn't known each other all that long, just felt right. And then the kiss when they said good night. Wow, totally hot.

The more time I spend with Matthew, the more I want to know him better. I'm still not sure that this will turn into anything long-term, but he certainly seemed interested last night.

He felt his eyes getting heavy again, so he closed them, thinking about that kiss.

He was just starting to doze again when he felt the bus come to a stop. Opening his eyes, he saw that they had arrived back at the ship.

"Hey, sleepyhead." He nudged Matthew, releasing his hand. "Wake up. We're home."

"Oh, hey," Matthew murmured, sleep still evident in his voice. "Wow, I was really out. Did you sleep too?"

"A little, but I woke up a few minutes ago." They rose and made their way off the bus.

They met up with the others in line to get back on the ship. Sam was saying something about stopping somewhere for a drink once they were aboard.

"I think I'm just gonna head to my cabin," Neil said. "I napped a little on the ride back but not as much as I would have liked. I might lie down for a bit."

"I'm going to my cabin too," said Matthew.

Neil saw Sam smile slightly and look at Julie, but all she said was, "Well, if you change your mind, we'll be at the Trident Lounge on Deck 8. I think Marco said he was working this afternoon, and he makes a great cosmopolitan."

As they ambled down the hallway to their respective suites, Neil looked over at Matthew. "Do you have any plans for dinner tonight?"

"Not really. After that lunch today, I was thinking of keeping it light." Matthew smiled shyly. "Did you have something in mind?"

"We could give Neptune's a try if you like. Wine and tapas?"

"That sounds great. What time?"

"I don't know how busy it gets, but I'll reach out to one of our Ocean Navigators to see if we need a reservation or anything. I'll text you."

"Sounds good." They had reached Matthew's door, and he stopped, looking up and down the corridor. Not seeing anyone about, he leaned forward and kissed Matthew tenderly. "See you later."

ONCE IN HIS CABIN, Neil opened the NavigatorChat app and sent a text to Stewart, one of the Ocean Navigators assigned to their suites. They'd met on the first day of the cruise, and he seemed eager to help them with anything they might need.

> Hi, Stewart. This is Neil Watkins in Suite 12116. Matthew Palmer and I are interested in having tapas for dinner in Neptune's tonight. Wasn't sure if we needed reservations or not. If we do, is something around eight o'clock possible? Thanks.

While he waited for a reply, he toed off his shoes and removed his shirt and jeans. He wanted to lie down and rest for a little while, so he set an alarm on his phone for two hours later. As he placed the phone on his nightstand, it buzzed; Stewart had responded.

> Hi, Neil. Reservations aren't typically needed, but I've gone ahead and secured a table for you at eight. I'll meet you and Matthew at your suites at seven forty-five to escort you to Neptune's. Let me know if you need anything else.

Well, that was easy.

He quickly sent Matthew a text with the details and lay down on the extremely comfortable mattress. Before long, he was fast asleep.

WHEN HE WOKE UP, he went to sit out on the balcony, enjoying the sunshine and sipping some prosecco; he had found a few small bottles of the sparkling wine in his mini fridge. The nap had been exactly what he needed; he felt refreshed and more than ready to spend some time with Matthew. He had donned a pair of shorts before venturing outside but was shirtless and relished the sun's warmth on his chest. They were still in port but were scheduled to leave in about an hour.

He heard a noise to his left and looked over. Matthew was standing in the break between their balconies. "Do you mind if I join you?"

"Of course not. That's why I texted you when I woke up." Neil lifted his glass. "There's some prosecco in the refrigerator if you're thirsty."

"Thanks." Matthew scooted into Neil's cabin and returned shortly with a flute of the wine. "*Cin cin.*" He sipped. "I don't know many Italian words, but at least I can toast like a native."

"Did you manage to sleep any more?" Neil scratched absently at the hair on his belly.

"Not really. I mean, I tried, but I guess the nap on the ride back was enough for me. I read for a while." He drank some more wine, then turned to Neil. "Thanks for sending me that list of books and authors. I've already bought a few and look forward to reading them."

"You're welcome. It's always nice to add another fan to our little group."

They were quiet for a few moments. The way the ship was docked, their balconies faced the water, and they both gazed out over the sapphire sea.

"Um, there's something I wanted to talk to you about, Matthew."

"Oh, that sounds a bit ominous." Matthew laughed nervously.

"Not really; I guess I'm just not quite sure how to start."

"Okay," Matthew said. "Take a deep breath, have another sip of wine, and just go for it."

Neil sighed. But he did exactly what Matthew suggested.

"I guess the best way to say it is, it's about us."

"Us?"

"Well, yeah. It seems like there might be something happening between us. We've kissed a couple of times, and we held hands on the ride back from Rome." Neil paused and tried to collect his thoughts. "Guess what I'm saying is that I like you, Matthew. A lot. And you seem interested in me."

"Yeah, I'm definitely interested in you." Matthew smiled.

"I'm not sure where this is going, but I'll tell you right now, I tend to have horrible luck meeting nice guys. I hope my luck is changing with you."

"Okay," Matthew said slowly. "To be honest, my track record with guys pretty much sucks too."

"Well, I'd like to get to know you better. You truly seem like a wonderful person. Do you want to see where this leads?"

"Yeah, I do. Of course, Rob, Ben, and Sam will be relentless if they find out about this. The three of them have been on my case for a while about dating again." He chuckled. "But what the hell? They're also the ones that pushed me hard to come on this cruise because I needed a change. I guess I can't blame them if they turn out to be right."

"I know what you mean. Ever since Kyle met Jon, he's been on me to find someone. But I have to be honest, I didn't expect to meet someone like you on this trip."

"Me neither. And hey, look at it this way, we may not end up together, but we'll get to know each other, and I'm pretty sure we'll become great friends even if it doesn't turn into more."

They clinked, drank, and emptied their glasses.

CHAPTER 9

Promptly at seven forty-five, the doorbell for Neil's suite rang. He had just finished dressing in stone-colored chinos and a cobalt-blue button-down shirt. He'd been told the hue of the shirt made his eyes seem even bluer, so why not play that up, right?

He opened the door, and sure enough, it was Stewart. His blond hair was styled in a quiff, and he wore the standard Ocean Navigator uniform of navy blazer, light-gray chinos, and a pale-teal shirt. A silver, teal, and sapphire Ocean Cruises logo pin adorned his lapel.

"Good evening, Neil." Stewart smiled broadly. "Are you ready?"

"Just about. I need to grab my phone, and then we can get Matthew."

A few moments later, they had retrieved Matthew, and the three of them proceeded to the elevator.

Stewart asked them about their day, and soon they were at Neptune's. He escorted them to a table for two in the corner, on the other side of the long mahogany bar. Removing the small brass RESERVED sign on the table, he addressed them both, "Enjoy your evening, gentlemen. Arturo will be here shortly with wine and tapas menus. If there's anything else I can do for you, please don't hesitate to contact me."

"Thank you." Neil shook Stewart's hand.

"Wow, I feel so spoiled on this vacation. Rob and Ben really went all out," Matthew said. "But I feel a little weird. I'm not used to having someone treat me like royalty."

"I know what you mean," Neil agreed. "But I decided that I'm just going to enjoy it while I can."

A waiter approached the table. "Good evening, gentlemen. My name is Arturo, and I'll be taking care of you tonight." He presented them with a wine list along with a tapas menu.

"Do you know what you'd like to drink, or do you need a few moments to review the wine list?"

Neil spoke up first. "I'd like a glass of the Carménère, please."

"That sounds good; I'll have the same."

"If you think you'd like more than one glass this evening, might I suggest getting a bottle?" Arturo asked.

Neil looked at Matthew, who nodded. "Yes, please."

"Very good, sir. Also, if there's something you're interested in that you don't see on the menu, please let me know as I may be able to get it for you. I'll be back with the wine momentarily."

"Oh, they have that tomato bread that we had at the seafood restaurant in Barcelona," Neil said, perusing the menu.

"Excellent, let's get some of that. Do they have shrimp?"

"Yeah. Grilled shrimp with herbs and lemon. And *jamón*. Hmmm, do you like oysters? I don't see them on the menu, but I know they have them in the seafood restaurant. Maybe Arturo can get some for us."

"Sure, that all sounds good. And maybe some cheese to go with the *jamón*?" Matthew asked.

"Yeah, they have a plate of cheese and olives."

"Okay, I think that'll be more than enough." Matthew laughed. "We said we were gonna keep this light."

"We did, but we can take our time and ask him to bring things out in stages."

"Perfect."

Arturo returned with their wine, and once it was opened and poured, they ordered. Arturo assured them he could get a dozen oysters for them and also set a leisurely pace for their meal.

As they waited for the first of the plates to arrive, Neil took a sip of wine and looked at Matthew. "What led you to become a jewelry designer?"

"Growing up, I always had an interest in artistic things. I loved to color and draw as a kid. My dad's an architect, so I think I got some of that from him. For a while, I thought I might follow in his footsteps." Matthew paused, looking quite pensive. Neil thought he was trying to gather his thoughts, so he waited patiently, just gazing at this stunning man.

"I guess I should say that the whole family is artsy. My older brother, Marcus, paints, mostly oils, but he does some things in acrylic too. Mom paints too, but her real love is fiber. She weaves and is especially fond of tapestry design. Micah, my younger brother, is an illustrator. He just started a new job in Boston for a rather large design firm." He smiled wistfully. "Seems like it was destiny that I ended up in some creative field."

Arturo delivered the oysters with an assortment of sauces and discreetly moved away. As they ate the delicious bivalves, Neil pressed on.

"So how did you end up moving from architecture to jewelry design?"

"Well, by the time I was ready for college, I had kind of switched gears. Architecture was a bit too technical for me, and I really didn't enjoy the engineering side of it all, so I focused more on illustration. That let me be a bit more creative."

He added some cocktail sauce to an oyster and slurped it from its shell before continuing.

"I went to the Rhode Island School of Design and on a whim took a jewelry class with a friend. I loved every part of it and shifted my focus to jewelry design. I still got a fair amount of illustration classes in, along with some pottery and sculpture, but it all feeds my love for jewelry."

"That's fascinating. I know that RISD is quite a prestigious school, so they obviously recognized your talent early on." Neil lifted the wineglass to his lips. After drinking a bit more of the ruby-hued liquid, he said, "And look at you now. You've got your own shop and design some amazing pieces."

"Thank you." Matthew lowered his eyes as if the praise embarrassed him. "I'm really happy with where I am in my career, but it wasn't easy." He paused, seeming to be unsure of how to continue.

"My folks weren't thrilled with my decision to switch to jewelry. I had come out to them a year earlier, and that had already put a strain on our relationship. I grew up in a very conservative Christian household. Neither of my folks were very supportive when I said I was gay, but Dad was especially disappointed. When I said I wanted to design jewelry, that was probably the final nail in the coffin."

"I'm so sorry, Matthew." Neil reached over and gently touched his hand.

"Thanks. It still hurts, but I've mostly learned how to deal with the pain. Mom's come around a bit but doesn't say too much so as not to rile up Dad. Shortly after I told them about my desire to switch my design focus, Dad started talking about conversion therapy and praying away the gay. It got to the point where I didn't feel safe in the house I grew up in, and with the help of my brothers, who are completely supportive of who I am, I moved out."

"Oh, Matthew!" Neil exclaimed. "I can't imagine what you went through."

"I won't lie. It was a tough few years. Fortunately, I had scholarships that covered most of my expenses. Plus, I worked whenever I could—nights, weekends, summers. And I survived."

"I'm so proud of what you've accomplished. And you should be too."

"Oh, I am. I'd developed a reputation of sorts by the time I graduated. People liked what I was doing with design, and through a school friend, I learned about a jewelry store in Westport that hired me. It was mostly retail sales stuff, but Charlie, the owner of the store, let me design a few simple pieces to sell at the shop. My popularity grew, and I got a little more daring in some of my designs. Eventually, Charlie retired, and I managed the place. He had no family and left the store to me when he died. I slowly changed it from a typical retail jewelry store to one that focuses on more eclectic designs and turned it into the Artistic Alchemist."

"Wow. That's an amazing story, Matthew." Neil lifted his glass in a toast. "Congratulations."

THE REST of their meal passed quite pleasantly. They'd taken their time and enjoyed the rest of the courses as they talked and drank more wine. Matthew shared a bit more about his love of design and what he was doing to keep the offerings at the shop fresh.

"Once I started shifting the focus of the shop, I knew I couldn't do it alone, but I also couldn't afford to hire several designers. I reached out to some of my friends from college and offered them a place to sell their work on consignment. Quite a few took me up on it, and I still have a couple of artists who continue to sell through my shop."

"That was a brilliant idea."

"Eventually, I was able to hire a couple of folks who create some simpler designs that we sell. That gives me time to focus on the custom work."

Arturo came over with a plate of fresh fruit. "Gentlemen, I know you didn't order this, but I thought you might like to end with something sweet. Is there anything else I can get for you?"

"Thank you so much, Arturo." Neil smiled graciously. "I'm fine; what about you, Matthew?"

"I don't need anything else either. Thank you."

As they nibbled on the beautiful strawberries, blueberries,

and melon, Neil thought about their earlier conversation. Matthew was an amazing, kind, and generous man. He'd been hesitant to spend time talking about himself, and he was glad they'd focused on Matthew tonight. He knew that Ben and Rob wouldn't be friends with a jerk, but it was nice to learn about Matthew this way—just the two of them.

"I'm so glad we decided to spend this time together, Matthew. I've learned so much about how wonderful you are. Thank you for sharing."

"You're very welcome." Matthew smiled, but it seemed a bit melancholy. "You're very easy to talk to, and I'm sorry if I brought down the conversation a bit when I talked about my dad. I try not to let him get to me anymore, but some days it's not easy."

"Nonsense. If anything, it made me see more of who you are. I'm just sorry that your parents can't see the real you."

Neil and Matthew stood and made their way up to the pool deck, where they strolled around for a little while, their shoulders occasionally brushing against each other as they made their way around the deck. Neil had been surprised to see they'd been talking for more than two hours over dinner.

The breeze had picked up a bit, and Matthew shivered.

"Are you cold? We should probably go back inside."

"Yeah, just a little bit," Matthew said sheepishly. "I forgot that we're underway now, and it's rather chilly."

When they reached Matthew's door, Neil turned to him. "I like you a lot, Matthew, and part of me wants to invite myself in or ask you back to my cabin." He smiled shyly. "But I'm not going to. I want to take this slowly because you're special and deserve to be treated that way."

Matthew grinned.

"I'll just say good night. I'm looking forward to our day in Florence tomorrow."

Neil leaned forward and kissed Matthew tenderly. They kissed again, but before things got too heated, Matthew broke the kiss.

"Thank you for this evening, Neil. I really enjoyed it. I love spending time with you."

CHAPTER 10

Thursday, October 13, Naples, Italy

Matthew opened his eyes just minutes before the alarm went off. Yes, his bladder definitely had a role in that, but he was excited too. The ship was in Naples, and he was spending a good part of the day with Neil.

Yesterday had been a fun day in Florence and Pisa; their entire group had booked the same tour, so they'd been together all day. He really did enjoy their company, but since he and Neil had connected a few days earlier, he found himself wanting to spend more time with only him. He'd get to do that today.

Most of the folks in their little group were heading off to Pompeii for an excursion, but he and Neil had decided on a walking tour of Naples.

He picked up his phone and sent off a quick text.

Wanna meet for breakfast?

Moments later, he got a reply.

Sure. How about 20 minutes?

Perfect.

That settled, he quickly showered and dressed. He was just slipping into his sneakers when his doorbell rang.

Neil looked stunning in a pale-blue polo and dark jeans.

"G'morning, handsome," Neil said when Matthew opened the door. "Are you ready?"

"One sec. Come in while I get my phone."

But instead of walking to the nightstand, Matthew leaned in and kissed Neil soundly on the mouth. He slipped his arms around Neil's shoulders and hugged him tightly.

"Can we just skip the tour and stay on the ship today?" Neil was breathless.

"No, but we should be back on board long before the rest of our group. I'm sure we'll think of something to pass the time later." He smirked.

THEY WERE ESCORTED off the ship by a crew member and met their guide, Matteo, a short distance from it. There were fewer than twenty people on their tour, and everyone seemed happy that their group was as small as it was.

The group walked to the Piazza Giovanni Bovio, and Matteo explained that the stock exchange building overlooked the piazza. Matthew snapped photo after photo, trying to capture the flavor of the city. He was fascinated by the architecture; so much of it was very ornate, with sculptures adorning the areas above the windows in many cases.

"It's amazing how much effort they made to make the buildings look like this. The craftsmanship is amazing," he effused.

"That it is," Neil agreed, taking his own photos along the way.

They visited a few churches, and several people in their group marveled at how ornate they were, both inside and out.

As they walked along, Matteo spoke about their next stop.

"Shortly we will arrive at Via San Gregorio Armeno. This is one of the most famous streets in all of Naples," he explained. "There are many shops here that specialize in creating what we call the cribs. They are the Nativity scenes; we are famous for those here in Napoli. We will take a short break here for perhaps thirty minutes so you can look around and shop if you wish."

He paused and pointed down a small side street.

"Here we are; you may walk down here and look around. Please come back to this spot in half an hour, and I will be waiting for you. Once you are all back, we will visit a pizzeria nearby for lunch before we make our way back to the ship."

They strolled leisurely down the narrow street, stopping occasionally to admire the craftsmanship of the work they saw. Matthew had never seen such a vast array of cribs in his life.

"This is unbelievable!" he exclaimed. "There are so many Nativities of all shapes and sizes."

After visiting several shops along the way, Matthew decided on a small Nativity set.

"I'm going to get this for my mom. If she were here, she'd be oohing and aahing over everything and would probably want something larger, but I like this one as it's a bit simpler in design."

The set he'd chosen was hand-carved wood, left in its natural finish.

"I'm not the most religious person," Neil admitted, "but it is beautiful. I'm sure she'll love it." He made his purchase, then they ambled along the street back to the meeting spot.

The pizzeria was housed in a beautiful old stone building. The group was led to a small courtyard on the far side, where they were seated at a mix of tables for two and four. It was a beautiful, sunny day, and it felt good to sit outdoors. There was a gentle breeze and a few umbrellas as well as some trees on the edge that kept the sun from beating down on them.

A couple of waiters wound their way through the tables, filling water glasses and setting down bottles of red and white wine.

Matthew lifted both bottles and asked, "Red or white?"

"Red, I think," replied Neil.

Neil sipped from the small, fluted tumbler, no fancy-stemmed wine glasses here, and nodded appreciatively. "Wow, that's really good."

"It is," Matthew agreed. "Do you think we'll get a choice of pizza, or will everyone just get a slice or two of whatever they're making?"

Neil glanced over at a door into the restaurant as a waiter walked out carrying a pizza in each hand.

"I think we're just getting whatever they're making." He pointed to the waiter as he placed the pizzas at a table of four across from them. "But if I'm not mistaken, everyone is getting their own pizza."

Sure enough, the next waiter walked up to their table and set a large pizza down in front of each of them.

"Oh my god, this looks fantastic," uttered Matthew. It was a simple pizza with tomato sauce, cheese, and a scattering of freshly torn basil leaves. The aroma was heavenly.

Neil noticed that the pizza was not cut into wedges like it would be at home.

"I remember Ben saying that they eat pizza with a knife and a fork here in Italy." That said, they picked up their utensils and began eating, relishing each savory bite.

"This is absolutely the best pizza I've ever eaten," Matthew said after chewing and swallowing. "It's so simple but utterly delicious."

"I agree. It's no wonder Naples is credited with inventing pizza. It's like no other pizza I've ever had."

Conversation waned as they both ate and drank.

"Whew, that's it for me." Matthew pushed his plate away. He'd managed to consume a little more than half of his pie.

"I'm stuffed too, but I want to keep eating because it's so good," Neil said. "Must. Stop. Eating." He looked at Matthew, and they both laughed.

Waiters quickly cleared tables and returned moments later with small slices of yellow cake and fresh strawberries. Despite protests of being too full to eat anything more, they both managed to finish most of the dessert.

"I'm really glad we have more walking to do. I really need to work this off."

"Truth."

It was almost three o'clock by the time they got back to the ship. They both felt better after the return walk, but Matthew thought a nap might be in order.

"What are you going to do now?" he asked Neil as they walked up the gangway. "The rest of our group aren't scheduled to be back from Pompeii until around six."

"Not sure. What about you?"

"I was thinking of taking a nap." He hesitated, not sure if he should say what was on his mind. *Ah, fuck it, the worst that can happen is that he says no.* "So, um, would you like to join me?" He smiled shyly.

"You mean take a nap with you? Are you sure? Don't get me wrong, I'd love to, but I don't wanna rush you." Neil grinned.

"I wouldn't have asked if I wasn't ready. How about this? We'll each go back to our cabins, and I'll open the sliders on the balcony. You can come over when you're ready."

"Sure," Neil agreed. "I'll drop off my stuff and probably change into shorts and a T-shirt so that I'm more comfortable, but I should be over in about ten or fifteen minutes."

They parted ways at the door to Matthew's suite with a brief kiss. "See you in a few."

Once inside his cabin, Matthew stripped and took a quick shower, then brushed his teeth. He stepped into a pair of lime-green trunks, then put on his navy sleep shorts and a gray T-shirt.

He sat on the edge of the bed, trying to slow his breathing. He was both excited and nervous at the prospect of lying in the same bed with Neil. They might not do much more than make out, but Matthew wanted to take the next step. "I can do this," he told himself, repeating it slowly, almost like a mantra. With each breath, he relaxed even more.

After a few minutes, he opened the sliding doors and stepped out onto the balcony.

He gazed out over part of the city of Naples, catching a glimpse of one of the churches they'd visited that morning. A noise to his right caused him to turn his head. The sight of Neil heading toward him took his breath away.

The man was stunning, even dressed in red-plaid sleep shorts and a white tank top. Matthew felt his mouth start to water. A smattering of dark hair poked up from the collar of Neil's shirt and covered his athletic arms and legs. His piercing blue eyes twinkled as if he knew Matthew was checking him out

He hugged Matthew soundly. "Hi, handsome."

"Hi, yourself." Matthew coughed, his mouth suddenly dry.

"Are you okay?" There was concern in Neil's voice.

"Yeah, I just need some water, I think."

Neil followed him into the suite and waited as Matthew sipped from a bottle he retrieved from the fridge. Setting the bottle down on the counter, he took Neil's hand and led him into the bedroom.

They lay facing each other as Matthew lightly stroked the hair at the top of Neil's chest.

"I really like this. A lot," he said quietly. "I've never really had much body hair but really appreciate a guy who does."

Neil smiled. "Would you like to see more?" he teased.

"Yes, please."

Neil pulled off the tank, and Matthew stared unashamedly. Pulling off his own shirt, he moved toward Neil and hugged him closer. He sighed, loving the feel of Neil's hairy chest against him.

Matthew kissed him, and when Neil opened to him, Matthew plunged his tongue in, tasting and teasing.

Neil suckled on Matthew's tongue, and Matthew felt himself start to harden against Neil's thigh. Running his hands down Neil's back, he grabbed at his ass and pulled. Neil moved slightly, and Matthew could feel his erection nestle along his now hard cock.

They continued to kiss and tease for several minutes, frotting against each other.

"I want to taste you," Matthew panted.

Neil nodded, so Matthew slowly kissed down the length of Neil's chest. When he reached his navel, he dipped his tongue in and grabbed the waistband of Neil's shorts. Neil lifted his ass, and Matthew pulled down the shorts and underwear in one smooth motion.

Neil's rigid dick slapped against his belly, and Matthew leaned in and sucked the head, then slicked down his length and nuzzled his hirsute balls, inhaling deeply.

"I love that you don't shave down here," Matthew said breathlessly. He returned to his ministrations, sucking each orb into his mouth, then running his tongue along the underside of Neil's weeping cock. He gathered up the pre-cum at the slit and swallowed it greedily, then took Neil's entire length into his throat.

Neil moaned, then pulled Matthew up and kissed him deeply. "We need to slow down a bit, or this will be over way too soon." Reaching down, he slipped his hands into the back of Matthew's shorts and kneaded his ass. After a moment, he lowered Matthew's shorts and briefs.

Staring at Matthew's thick, heavy cock, he said, "Mmmm, I need to taste that."

He maneuvered around so that he was facing Matthew's dick while his crotch was now at Matthew's eye level. Slowly, he began to lick around the flared head.

Matthew groaned as he lapped at Neil's length, stroking as he sucked the head into his mouth.

Neil licked Matthew's smooth balls and sighed. Licking up his long cock, he tickled under the crown with the tip of his tongue.

Matthew wet the tip of his middle finger with saliva, then moved his hand behind Neil's sac as he continued to suck his dick. He rubbed across his hole, circling the puckered entrance.

He heard Neil moan and pushed in slightly. Neil's legs spread a bit, so he moved in farther. Using his tongue to add more saliva into the mix, he continued to finger fuck him while he sucked his cock.

"Not gonna last," Neil panted. "So good."

"That's the whole point," Matthew said. "Come for me, baby."

Pushing in even more, he felt Neil's balls tighten, and his mouth was suddenly filled with Neil's release. He swallowed as fast as he could but felt a bit dribble from his lips.

He sensed Neil speed up his licking and sucking and couldn't stop the orgasm that tore through him.

After a few moments, Matthew's breathing slowed, and Neil flipped around so that he was facing Matthew. They kissed, licking cum from each other's mouths and moaning together as their spend mingled with their kiss.

"That was amazing," Neil said breathlessly.

"It was." Matthew tried unsuccessfully to stifle a yawn.

"Is it okay if we cuddle?" Neil smiled and kissed Matthew on the nose. "I think we've both earned a nap."

"Oh, yeah. I love cuddling."

Matthew turned, and they spooned, quickly drifting off.

MATTHEW WOKE with a cock nestled along his crack and an arm across his belly. He smiled at the memory of what he and Neil had done before their nap. There were no feelings of regret, only a sense of warmth filling him. Neil was a good guy, and he was happy that they'd decided to pursue whatever this was that they were feeling.

Picking up his phone from the nightstand, he saw that it was just past six—wow, they were out for longer than he had expected. But nature called, so he gently moved Neil's arm and quietly tiptoed into the bathroom. He was washing his hands when Neil stepped in and pointed to the toilet.

"May I?"

"Be my guest."

Neil peed and joined him at the sink, kissing his shoulder and meeting his eyes in the mirror.

"How are you feeling?" Neil asked, a look of concern on his face.

"Sated." Matthew smiled warmly.

"No regrets?"

"None whatsoever. I'm glad we acted on our feelings, and for what it's worth, I'd love to do that"—he paused, and his smile turned just a bit wicked—"and more with you again."

Relief flooded Neil's face.

"I'm glad too. I like you a lot, Matthew, and more sounds wonderful. But I think maybe food is in order first."

"Yes. What would you like?" They both checked their phones but had no waiting messages from the rest of their group.

"How about room service?" Matthew asked.

"That sounds great," Neil agreed. "Maybe Stewart could get us food from the steak house?"

'Great idea." Matthew pulled up the menu for the Seahorse Steakhouse, and they decided on a few items, then Matthew texted Stewart and asked if that was something he could take care of.

A few moments later, their Ocean Navigator replied that everything was taken care of and that dinner would be delivered at eight fifteen.

"How about a shower while we wait?" Matthew asked.

"You have the best ideas."

After dinner they sat out on the balcony, sharing a lounge chair and sipping drinks.

"Today was the best day ever," Matthew said. "Thanks for spending it with me."

"I had a great time too. I'm not exactly sure what's happening between us, but I like it, and I'd like to see where it goes."

"Me too," Matthew agreed. "This might sound corny, but from the moment we met, you seemed special. I swear I felt an electric shock when we shook hands at Rob and Ben's home."

"Wait. You felt that too? I thought it was just me. Nothing

like this has ever happened to me, but I can't ignore this feeling."

"It won't be easy. I mean, we live about four hundred miles away from each other, but I do want to try."

"I do too." Neil paused. "So, what do we tell the others? I can't really keep anything from Kyle, so he's bound to suspect something."

"And there's not getting anything past Sam. She's likely to take one look at us and know. It's like her superpower or something."

Matthew considered and realized that he wasn't afraid of letting people know about him and Neil. Neil was a good guy, and they definitely had feelings for each other. It was nothing to be ashamed of.

"I don't care who knows," Matthew admitted.

"Neither do I. If anyone asks, we can just say that something clicked between us, and we're seeing what happens. Does that work for you?"

"Yeah, it does. I really don't think anyone's going to care."

At that moment, Matthew's phone rang.

"Well, speak of the devil," he said as he glanced at the screen.

"Hi, Sam. I had a great day, thanks. Neil and I did the walking tour, and then we hung out in my cabin when we got back to the ship."

Neil smiled at Matthew and nodded.

"Actually, we got room service delivered, and now we're sitting on the balcony watching the stars."

After a moment, he said, "We're fine, and I'm sure we'll see you tomorrow. Good night."

"She knows, right?" Neil asked.

"Well, she didn't come out and say anything specific, but I think it's safe to assume that she suspects something. I predict that by tomorrow, everyone in our little group will know."

"That's fine. I guess I'd rather folks know than think that we're trying to hide something. Which clearly, we're not."

"Well then, would you like to stay over tonight?"

"Funny, I was thinking the same thing."

CHAPTER 11

Neil woke, feeling better than he had in a very long time. For the most part, he loved his life. He enjoyed his job and had some good friends, especially Kyle. He and Kyle had been besties for several years now, and it kind of surprised him how that had all worked out.

They'd met at work, having started at the investment company at the same time, so they naturally gravitated to each other as the new guys. He'd liked Kyle immediately. He was a no-nonsense kind of guy, and something just clicked between the two of them.

When they realized that they were both interested in men—well, Kyle had dated both men and women, but whatever—they'd even tried dating but quickly decided that they were better as friends than lovers. And when Kyle met Sam's cousin Jon last year, Neil was thrilled for him because Kyle deserved happiness, and Jon definitely made him happy. But he also felt a little sad that he couldn't seem to find the right guy. Perhaps his luck was finally changing.

He turned over to see Matthew looking at him, brown eyes staring warmly.

"G'morning." Matthew's voice had a tinge of sleepiness in it.

"Hi, handsome."

"How'd you sleep?"

"Really well," Neil replied. "How about you?"

"Can't remember when I had a better night's rest."

After they'd showered, Neil, clad in just a towel wrapped around his waist, walked across the balcony to his own suite to put on fresh clothes.

A few minutes later, as they walked to the elevator, Matthew said, "How do you feel about PDAs?"

"I'm fine with them, why?"

"Good to know." Matthew reached for Neil's hand. "So this is okay?"

"More than okay, but are you sure you're ready to go public about us?"

"I am," Matthew replied. "You're not having second thoughts, are you?"

"Not at all." Neil tightened his grip on Matthew's hand. "But once someone in our group sees us, everybody's gonna know."

"Perfect. And Sam's most likely already figured it out, so the cat's probably outta the bag anyway."

When they approached the hostess at the Bluefin Bistro, she said, "Good morning, gentlemen. I believe there are some others from your group already seated. Would you like to sit with them?"

"If it's not too much trouble, that would be great," Neil said.

"Not a problem at all, sir. The table next to them is empty, so I'll just move it over."

Sam, Julie, and Jon were sitting at a table near the window. The hostess and a passing waiter quickly moved the table so Matthew and Neil could sit down.

"Good morning, boys," Sam greeted them, pointedly staring at their joined hands. "I guess yesterday was a really good day, huh?"

"Good morning, everyone. And yes, Sam, it was a great day. Neil and I had a wonderful time, and we've decided to stop ignoring whatever this is that we feel for each other." Matthew smiled at Neil. "We're not sure where this will lead, but we've decided to give it a shot."

"Not that you need my approval, but I'm happy for you. You both deserve a nice guy in your lives."

"Thanks, Sam. And not to change the subject, but where's Kyle?" he asked, looking at Jon.

"He forgot his phone in the cabin. You were probably in an elevator, and if I know Kyle, he took the stairs down to our room." He sipped his coffee and looked up. "Ah, here he is now."

Kyle sat, smiling. "Hi, guys. What's going on?"

"Matthew and Neil have decided to become a couple," Sam effused. "Isn't that great?"

"Oh my god, that's wonderful," Kyle said, beaming. "Congrats."

THEY WERE SITTING TOGETHER near one of the many windows in the Lighthouse Lounge, gazing out at what seemed to be an endless azure sea. The lounge was located on the uppermost deck of the ship and offered spectacular panoramic views.

"Whatcha thinking?" Matthew asked, reaching for Neil's hand.

"About how strange life can be sometimes." Neil paused, trying to gather his thoughts. "I don't think I've slept around a lot or anything, but I'm no virgin either. And I've not really had much luck meeting nice guys. Well, until now, that is." He smiled, stroking his thumb along the back of Matthew's hand.

"I guess I'm thinking about how this is gonna work."

"Hey, don't worry about that now," Matthew said, tenderness in his tone. "We can figure shit out as we move forward. But that's all for another day. Now … I've managed to spill my guts about my crazy family. Why don't you tell me a little bit more about you?"

"Okay. I grew up in Virginia, a small town called Wytheville. My mom and sister still live there. Dad passed away when I was a teenager."

"I'm sorry. That must have been a difficult time for you."

"It was, but Mom did a great job holding us all together. My sister, Cheryl, is married and has three great kids, who of course, adore their uncle Neil."

"Of course, they do. And I can totally see why." Matthew's eyes shone brightly.

"Mom never remarried, but she seems happy with her life at this point. She pushed both Cheryl and me to pursue our dreams. I know Cheryl is happy with her life. She became an accountant and works part-time, mostly during tax season. Her husband, Philip, is a banker. I guess I'm happy for the most part. I like my job, but frankly, I'm not sure if I see myself staying there forever. We'll see."

Neil paused, wondering how to continue.

"And how have you managed to stay single?" Matthew asked, smiling warmly.

"I've had absolutely no luck meeting guys. Well, until now." He blushed shyly.

"That seems odd to me since you're a great guy. Care to trade horror stories?"

"Sure, but fair warning, it's not gonna be pretty."

"Ha." Matthew laughed. "Mine aren't either. Bring it."

"So, last December I had taken a few extra days off before the holidays so I could finish my shopping. My plan was to leave Wednesday morning to drive to my mom's house. I'd been seeing this guy, Tristan, for a few months and had agreed to meet him for brunch at a local restaurant on that Tuesday since we wouldn't be seeing each other for Christmas." Neil shook his head. "I still can't believe this happened. We were having mimosas, and I was telling him about what Christmas with the Watkins clan was like, when this striking blonde woman walked up to our table and said, 'Is this why you couldn't stay last night, Tris? Didn't want to be late for brunch with him?'"

"Oh my god, really?" Matthew said, mouth agape. "Why do I feel it's about to get worse?"

Neil nodded. "Tristan started to say, 'But baby, I can explain ...' But she cut him off, slapped him across the face, threw what was left of his mimosa at him, and practically shrieked, 'The engagement is off!' as she stormed out of the restaurant."

"What? Oh, fuck! I'm so sorry, Neil."

"Needless to say, I got up as calmly as I could and walked out. Sure, we hadn't been seeing each other for all that long and weren't really exclusive or anything, but a fiancée? Really? The fact that he was bi didn't matter, but an engagement usually means you're not seeing anyone else, right?"

"I can't imagine something like that."

"He tried to call me, but I ignored his calls and texts and deleted him from my contact list. I mean, nothing he was gonna say would change what happened."

Neil paused to take a sip of water from the bottle he had with him.

"I've had a few dates since then but never more than a couple with the same guy. Nothing really seemed to click with anyone I've met. And the last guy I went out with,"—he shook his head—"oh my god, don't even ask."

"Well, I can see where that experience with Tristan might put you off guys for a while," Matthew uttered quietly.

"Okay, your turn."

"The last serious relationship I had ended a few years ago. His name is Stephen, and we were together for a couple of years. At one point early on, I actually thought he might be the one."

He stopped, and Neil got a little concerned.

"Hey, if this is too difficult, you don't need to go on. No pressure at all."

"No, it's okay. I want to tell you. I guess I'm just trying to figure out how to tell it." He took a deep breath and pushed on.

"He lived in Dartmouth, which is the next town over from Westport. We met at a gay bar in a nearby city, and at first, he seemed like a dream come true. Handsome, successful—he was a professor of economics at a university in the area."

He shook his head as if remembering how it all started.

"He was out and brought me to staff functions and such. Looking back on it all now, I sometimes wonder if he was trying to impress the people he worked with because he was dating a guy of color. At the time, I didn't feel it, but now I sometimes think that might have been the case."

"Oh, Matthew. I'm so sorry. That really sucks."

"And as time went on, he started talking about trying to get a better job in a bigger city—New York or Boston or Chicago. But I was just getting my business going. This all happened right after Charlie died, and I was trying to rebrand my jewelry business. Stephen was trying to pressure me to sell it and move to a better place—his words—so that he could be recognized for his talents."

He reached for the bottle of water in Neil's hand. "May I?"

"Of course." Neil opened the bottle and handed it to him.

He took a long sip and handed the bottle back. "Thanks."

"Stephen couldn't understand why I wanted to stay in a small town. He kept saying we could both be so much more in a big city. He didn't grasp the fact that it was never my dream. Over time, he got verbally abusive about it all. Telling me I was a coward, afraid to take a chance in the big leagues."

"I'm so sorry, Matthew. He sounds like a real jerk."

Matthew chuckled humorlessly. "He was. I was good friends with Sam and Rob at the time, and I confided in them because I wasn't sure what to do. The pressure that Stephen was putting on me was getting to be too much. They agreed that if Stephen couldn't or wouldn't see what I wanted, then we should probably part ways."

"I'm really glad you had them in your life to help you through that."

"Me too. They really are family to me. Anyway," he continued, "I told Stephen how I felt and that I wasn't ready to move away from Westport—at least not then—and he freaked out. He berated me for not wanting to take a risk and called me a fool among other things. Told me that if I was just going to be a coward all my life, maybe I should do the world a favor and just end it all. It was an ugly breakup, and he did his best to convince mutual friends that I was an idiot. Thankfully, most of them didn't believe him."

"Wow. That was harsh. He sounds like a real dick." Neil paused, wondering what to say next. "So, you said that he was a professor; did he end up moving away?"

"Yeah. I broke off all contact with him, but I heard that he moved to New York. Not sure where he is or what he's doing, and frankly, I don't care. Since then I'm pretty much like you. A few dates here and there, but nothing ever seems to stick."

Neil took his hand and squeezed lightly. "I think we're both better off for what we've been through. Maybe we were just waiting to finally meet each other."

"You may be right," Matthew agreed. "I don't know about you, but I could use something stronger than water right now, and this bar doesn't open until later. How about we head down to Seaside Cove and find something there?"

"You have the best ideas."

Hand in hand, they walked toward the elevators.

AFTER A COUPLE of drinks with Matthew at the Mermaid's Tail pub, Neil was back in his cabin for a quick nap before dinner.

What is it about being on a ship that makes me want to doze every afternoon? he wondered.

His phone buzzed. Thinking it was Matthew, he picked it up off the nightstand and was surprised to see a text from Kyle.

> Hey! My dad has a table reserved at the Bluefin Bistro for dinner at seven thirty. Please join us.

He quickly typed a response.

> Sure. Can I ask Matthew?

> Absolutely.

Dinner plans settled, he fell asleep.

His alarm woke him ninety minutes later, and he sent off a quick text to Matthew about dinner, then jumped in the shower.

A few minutes later, wearing only a towel, he was standing in front of his closet, trying to decide what to wear to dinner. He heard a knock on the balcony sliding doors, and there he found Matthew, looking stunning in black slacks and a magenta shirt.

"Hey there." He leaned in for a kiss. "Come in."

"Is this what you're wearing to dinner tonight?" Matthew smiled innocently.

"Don't be a smart-ass. I was just trying to decide what to wear when you knocked."

As he turned to walk back into the bedroom, Matthew

grabbed the towel, and Neil was left standing there naked. He felt his look of shock suddenly turn sly, and he said, "Come help me decide."

After a few more kisses, Matthew pulled Neil closer, grabbing his ass cheeks with both hands.

"As much as I'd love to continue this line of thinking, we really shouldn't keep our hosts waiting." Neil's growing excitement was evident as he pulled away from Matthew.

"You're right, but maybe I can help take care of that later."

"I think we can make that happen," Neil said as he slipped into a pair of cobalt-blue trunks. Dressing quickly in navy slacks and a white button-down shirt, he grabbed his phone, and they left for the restaurant.

They followed the hostess to the table where Ben, Rob, Sam, Jon, and Kyle were seated.

"Hi, everyone," Matthew greeted them. "Thanks for the invitation."

"Of course," replied Rob. "We hadn't seen you guys for a while and thought it would be nice to get together."

"Sam, where's Julie?" Matthew asked.

"She had a headache earlier and decided to take it easy tonight. She got some room service and was planning on going to bed early."

"I hope she's feeling better in the morning," Neil said.

"And before we forget," Ben began, "we want to invite you to lunch tomorrow in Mykonos. I'll send out a text with all the details, but there's a great place that Rob's been going to for quite a while. He introduced me to it last year, and we thought it would be nice to get the whole group together for a typical Greek meal."

Rob continued the thread, "Sam worked her magic and got us a reservation there at one o'clock tomorrow. Since we're in Mykonos until eight tomorrow night, we figured folks could take it easy in the morning, and we'll get off the ship around twelve thirty."

"That sounds great, thanks," Neil said. "I was thinking of checking out the Sanctuary at the Sapphire Spa tomorrow morning. They have a hydrotherapy pool, steam room, and sauna."

"Jon and I were talking about that earlier," Kyle added. "We're most likely going too."

"That sounds good to me," Sam said enthusiastically. "Matthew, are you interested in joining us?"

"Sure. What time do we want to go?"

"How about nine thirty?" Jon offered. "We can spend about an hour there and still have plenty of time to get ready for lunch after that."

"Dad, Rob? How about you guys? Want to join us in the spa?"

"Thanks, but we're planning on sleeping in tomorrow," Ben said, a twinkle in his eye. "After all, it is our honeymoon."

They all laughed, and the conversation turned to what to order for dinner.

It was late when they got back to Neil's cabin. Dinner had seemed to go on for hours, with lively conversation and much laughter. And it didn't help that Ben kept ordering more wine.

As soon as the door shut behind them, Matthew pushed Neil against the door and kissed him roughly, pushing his tongue into Neil's mouth and moaning.

Neil felt Matthew's hand travel down his torso and rub against his growing cock.

"Been wanting this all evening," Matthew panted as he unbuttoned Neil's slacks and sank to his knees.

Tucking Neil's trunks behind his balls, he licked at the flared head of Neil's dick, running his tongue along the frenulum.

"Ungh," Neil moaned, not able to control himself. "Not gonna last if you keep that up."

"That's the whole point," Matthew said between licks.

"I'd like to get in on some of the action," Neil said breathlessly, pulling Matthew up and kissing him deeply.

They quickly stripped, moving to the bed, where they lay on their sides, mouth to dick, licking, sucking, teasing each other into a frenzy.

Matthew moved so that he hovered above Neil, taking his cock to the root.

Presented with Matthew's cock, balls, and gorgeous ass, Neil decided to be a bit daring and parted his cheeks, lapping at his smooth hole greedily.

"Oh my god," Matthew panted. "Don't stop."

Neil felt his balls tighten as Matthew continued to lick around the head of his cock.

"Gonna come," Neil cried out. Matthew covered Neil's cock head just as his orgasm hit.

Neil covered his finger with saliva and worked it into Matthew's hole, continuing to lick around the rim.

Matthew grunted, and Neil felt hot cum hit his upper chest as Matthew came.

As their breathing slowed, Neil groaned, "Wow, that was …"

"Yeah."

They stumbled into the bathroom and quickly showered.

Falling into bed, they spooned and were fast asleep within minutes.

CHAPTER 12

Saturday, October 15, Mykonos, Greece

Matthew kissed the back of Neil's neck and felt Neil push closer, nudging his back into Matthew's chest.

"Hey," Matthew said, kissing Neil's shoulder tenderly.

"Hey yourself, handsome. What time is it?"

"Dunno. And I'd have to move to find out."

"I have to pee, so I'll check." Neil lifted Matthew's arm and slipped from the bed, padding to the bathroom.

Matthew turned over but didn't see his phone on the nightstand. Sighing, he got up and started toward the living room.

As Neil returned to the bedroom, he said, "Have I told you lately that you have a magnificent ass?"

"No," Matthew called over his shoulder, "but feel free."

"You have a magnificent ass," Neil repeated.

Matthew bent over to pick up various articles of clothing that were strewn across the living room.

Neil groaned, bending over to plant a kiss on Matthew's right ass cheek. "You're killing me, dude."

Matthew chuckled.

Finding his phone on the sofa, Neil said, "It's seven thirty. We've got enough time to clean up and meet the gang for breakfast before going to the spa."

Matthew quickly dressed, kissed Neil on the lips, and headed to the door. "I'll be back in a few minutes."

Kyle, Jon, Neil, and Matthew were sitting at a table in the Bluefin Bistro when Sam and Julie joined them.

"Good morning, everyone," Sam said, sitting next to Matthew.

"Feeling better, Julie?" Neil asked.

"Yes, thanks. Laying low last night was exactly what I needed."

"Are you joining us at the spa, Julie?" Matthew smiled at her.

"No, I'll go sit somewhere and read for a bit, but I want to hear all about it when we get together for lunch."

They all selected light items—yogurt and fresh fruit, mostly—and dug in when their waiter returned with their choices.

Once at the front desk of the Sapphire Spa, they each checked in and received a locker key. Parting ways at the changing rooms, Sam said she'd meet them at the hydrotherapy pool.

Neil led the way into the men's locker room, where they located their respective lockers and changed into swimsuits. Each locker contained flip-flops and a plush robe, so they donned them and went in search of the Sanctuary area of the spa.

Sam was waiting on a lounge chair along one wall near the pool.

"Grab some towels over there and leave them here with your robes." She pointed to a shelf area near the entrance, lined with rolled-up towels.

The hydrotherapy pool was a large rectangular affair. Neil thought it looked like a hot tub on steroids. One wall contained a sitting area made of stainless-steel tubes that turned into a wide lounge of sorts, and bubbles flowed over and around the entire section.

There were also two waterspouts that looked like large faucets and a few other areas of concentrated bubble activity.

"This looks amazing," Neil said to no one in particular. There were no other passengers in the spa. Neil supposed it was because they were already docked, and lots of people were already getting off the ship.

They entered the pool and tried out the different options. The water was quite hot, but they got used to it quickly.

"Oh my god, this is heavenly," Jon uttered. He was standing under one of the faucet devices, letting the water pound across his back and shoulders.

Neil and Matthew settled in on the lounge space and let the bubbles work out tension along their shoulders, backs, and legs.

"I really want one of these at home," Neil joked.

After about ten minutes in the pool, Neil got out and went

to a door with a sign that explained it was the Laconicum room—a dry-heated room infused with different aromas that would help detoxify the body.

He stepped in and immediately felt the temperature change. It was warmer but not uncomfortably so. He sat on one of the benches that surrounded the room and willed himself to relax. Matthew and Kyle joined him a few minutes later.

"This just feels so good." Matthew sighed.

"It does," Kyle agreed. "We need to do this again before the end of the cruise."

After a few minutes, they all left and saw Jon leaving one of the other rooms.

"That one was too hot for me," he said to the group. "It was a bit difficult to breathe in there."

Between the two rooms was a bank of showers, each with a plaque describing their features. One was a tropical rain forest, with warm water from a large showerhead and side sprays.

Matthew stepped into one that was a cold-mist shower. As he pushed the button to start the water flowing, he was surrounded by a cool, invigorating mist, mixed with what was described as calming aromas. After the heat of the pool and the Laconicum room, it felt wonderful. It stopped after a few minutes, and he stepped out.

"You all have to try this one; it feels so good," he announced to the group.

They all took a turn and agreed it was refreshing after everything else.

They spent a little more time in the pool, then ended with the cool-mist shower once again.

Wrapped in towels, they sat on heated stone loungers and relaxed, placing cool facecloths over their eyes.

After about fifteen minutes, Sam spoke up. "I hate to break up this party, but we still need to shower and get ready to disembark."

Neil groaned. "You're right, but this has been fantastic. We definitely need to do it again."

Tossing their used towels in a hamper near the exit, they trudged back to the locker rooms to shower and change.

THE SIX OF THEM—KYLE, Jon, Matthew, Neil, Sam, and Julie—were leaving the ship when each of their phones buzzed.

Matthew was the quickest at pulling his phone from his front pocket and announced to the group, "It's from Ben. He and Rob are outside waiting for everyone to show up. We should take a right as we exit the ship and will see them near the water."

Sure enough, they saw Ben and Rob standing off to the side of the walkway.

"I just got a text from Mike," Ben began as the group approached them. "He, Ellen, Mike Jr., Becky, and Wyatt are on their way. They should be here in about five minutes."

"So how was the spa this morning?" Rob asked.

"It was amazing," Matthew effused. "We all agreed we need to do it again before the end of the cruise."

He was standing near Neil and unconsciously grabbed his hand. Neil turned to him and smiled. "Yeah, it was so relaxing. I might have said that I want a spa at home now."

"They are pretty nice," Rob agreed. "If you count our

dinner at the tapas restaurant two years ago as our first date, my second date with Ben was at a spa in Barcelona. We've actually thought about putting a sauna in at home."

Matthew saw Ben glance down to his hand holding Neil's.

"Am I correct in assuming that you two are seeing each other?" Ben asked, gesturing at their joined hands.

"Yeah," Matthew replied, blushing a bit. "We admitted that we were attracted to each other a couple of days ago, so we're seeing where this goes."

"Congrats," Ben said. "You're both great guys, so I hope things go well for you."

"Sam and I are gonna head to the restaurant now to make sure everything is set up," Rob told the group. "We'll see you in a few minutes."

Sam and Rob departed, and the rest of the group chatted about what to do after lunch while they waited for Mike and his family to arrive.

A few minutes later, Mike, Ellen, Mike Jr., and Becky arrived. Wyatt was in a BabyBjörn carrier on his dad's chest.

"Rob and Sam already went to the restaurant to ensure everything was ready," Ben announced. "It takes fifteen to twenty minutes to get there."

They strolled leisurely as a group, taking in the gorgeous scenery—azure waters, colorful boats bobbing in the harbor, and an assortment of cafes and tavernas along the road.

Eventually they came to a little restaurant called Mourayio. A small place tucked between two other eating establishments, it featured blue-and-white chairs and tables overlooking the harbor.

Sam and Rob were seated at a table on the right and called them over.

"We have these three tables," Sam announced to them. "We've ordered an assortment of food for each table, but we weren't sure what folks would want to drink, so feel free to order some beverages."

Julie and Ben joined Sam and Rob, Mike and his family took the second table, and Matthew, Neil, Kyle, and Jon grabbed the last one.

Waiters brought out platters of shrimp saganaki, moussaka, a regional salad, and spanakopita, depositing them at each table. Kyle ordered a beer called Alpha, and the other guys followed suit.

"Goodness, this is fantastic," Matthew exclaimed after tasting the shrimp.

They chatted between tables about which foods they liked best and had to agree that it was all delicious.

Once they'd eaten their fill, they thanked Ben and Rob profusely for the meal and then headed off in pairs or small groups to do a bit of exploring in town.

Matthew and Neil walked around the harbor until they reached a small church. They took photos, including a couple of selfies. It was a warm day, and Neil had dressed in off-white shorts and a salmon-hued T-shirt; Matthew couldn't take his eyes off him. *God, he looks especially handsome today.*

Following the road they were on, they turned occasionally so as to keep the water in sight on their right. Soon they turned a corner and saw a set of windmills on a slight hill. Reaching them, they found sweeping views of the Aegean Sea and their ship.

"This is magnificent," Matthew uttered, almost in awe. "I never could have imagined how beautiful it is here."

"I agree," Neil said. "I'd love to come back here someday and just spend a week enjoying it all."

Matthew pulled a small sketchbook out of his backpack. "I just want to sketch a couple of things, and then we can move on. I know I can take pictures, but sometimes it just feels right to make a quick sketch of something."

"Don't rush," Neil answered. "It's still early. We've got plenty of time."

After a few moments, Matthew flipped the book around to show Neil what he'd drawn. "What do you think?"

"Oh my god, that's fantastic!" Neil exclaimed.

Matthew had done a simple sketch of one of the windmills, paying special attention to the door and the pottery urn to its left, filled with plants and flowers.

"It's so simple, but you captured its essence beautifully."

Neil pulled out his phone and asked Matthew to stand near the door with his sketchbook. He took a photo and showed it to him. "I want to preserve this moment forever. Thanks for letting me be a part of it with you."

Matthew felt a bit overwhelmed. He was falling for this wonderful, thoughtful man and hoped that they could make it work. He was afraid his heart might not survive if they couldn't.

"Thank you," Matthew whispered, hugging Neil. "I'm so very happy that I'm here with you."

Stowing his book and pencil, Matthew said, "Okay, let's see what else we can find."

They turned a corner and were heading back toward the main part of the town when Neil grabbed his hand and started up a street to their right. It was narrow and had the typical whitewashed walls and brightly colored doors and shutters that were everywhere here. Mostly blue, but an occasional magenta or plum door stood out.

The road had a slight incline, and occasionally they would come upon a few steps to ease the ascent. After a few minutes of walking, they reached the top of the road, and as they turned to the left were presented with a fantastic view over-looking the city and harbor.

"Oh my god!" Matthew exclaimed. "This is spectacular."

They both pulled out their phones and snapped an array of photos. A nearby building, with the requisite azure door, had a beautiful spray of bougainvillea growing along one wall, and Matthew snagged a few close-up shots from different angles. Then just to be safe, he took a few more photos from a distance.

Turning his phone, he showed them to Neil.

"Those are fantastic, Matthew," he effused. "You should print those and frame them."

"I might just do that. Let's see if I can get some other shots along the way, and then we can choose the best ones."

"We can choose, huh?" Neil was grinning from ear to ear. "I like the sound of that."

"Remember, we cruise virgins are in this together."

They laughed and headed down the next street over, in search of more photo opportunities.

ABOUT AN HOUR LATER, they were back in front of Mourayio, and Ben and Rob were still sitting at their table, enjoying glasses of wine.

"Have you guys been sitting here all along?" Matthew queried.

"Yeah," answered Rob. "We thought about walking around but decided drinking wine and people watching was a nicer way to spend our time. Would you care to join us?"

"Thanks, that would be nice," replied Neil. "We've been walking all around taking photos. I could use a drink, I think."

"That sounds good," Matthew agreed. "I saw a sign for a beer called Mythos; I want to give that one a try."

Rob called over a waiter and ordered the beers.

"Did you see the windmills?" asked Ben.

"Yeah; they're beautiful. I think I got some nice shots." Matthew handed his phone to Ben.

As Ben scrolled through them, Rob looked on as well.

"Matthew, these are fantastic," Rob said. "Some of these are definitely worth framing."

"That's exactly what I told him," added Neil.

"You could probably even sell them in the shop if you wanted." Ben looked at him. "I believe people would pay for these."

"Hmmm, that's actually a pretty good idea," Matthew admitted. "I've been thinking about expanding the store's inventory. This could be it."

"Let us know when you decide to offer them." Ben nodded at Matthew. "We'll definitely make a purchase."

CHAPTER 13

Neil and Matthew were returning to their cabins after a lovely dinner at Waves. They'd eaten with Kyle and Jon and thoroughly enjoyed the fresh seafood the restaurant had to offer.

"I don't know what I liked more, the fresh oysters or the seafood Provençal." Neil rubbed his belly with satisfaction.

"I say it was a tie." Matthew sighed. "It was all so delicious. But I'm glad we decided to skip the nightcap with Kyle and Jon. I've been dying for some alone time with you all evening."

"So you'll spend the night with me?" Neil grinned.

"Absolutely. How about I go shower and change into something more comfortable and meet you on the balcony?"

"Perfect. See you in a few minutes."

A quick kiss at Matthew's door and Neil rushed down the hall to his own stateroom.

He stripped and quickly showered, donned a pair of navy sleep shorts, then quickly brushed his teeth and washed his face. Stepping out into the cool breeze on his balcony felt wonderful, and he marveled at the sight before him.

Matthew was standing at the railing, gazing out at the inky sea. Wide, deep-brown shoulders led to his trim waist and a magnificent ass clad in tight orange trunks.

Neil wrapped his arms around him, kissing his neck and shoulders and running his hands across Matthew's belly. "Hey, handsome," he whispered.

"Hey, yourself." Matthew leaned back, snuggling closer.

Stars filled the midnight sky, and Neil felt like the luckiest guy alive.

It's probably too soon, but I think I'm falling in love with this guy.

Matthew turned, and Neil felt his crotch press against his own. They kissed deeply, Matthew opening up to Neil's probing tongue.

Neil slipped his hands under the waistband of Matthew's shorts and squeezed his ass. He felt Matthew harden against his own growing erection.

With one last kiss, Neil sighed. "We should probably take this inside."

Once in the cabin, Matthew followed Neil into the bedroom, and they lay together, Neil on top of Matthew.

Matthew spread his legs slightly, and Neil frotted against him, relishing the feel of Matthew's cotton-covered cock against his own. He sucked Matthew's tongue into his mouth, moaning.

Breaking the kiss, Matthew panted, "Want you inside me."

"Are you sure?" Neil asked tenderly. "I want that too but no pressure."

"I'm ready," Matthew said. "Please."

Neil lowered Matthew's trunks, then removed his own shorts, and reaching into the bedside drawer, pulled out a condom and a small bottle of lube.

"Tonight's all about you," he said and slowly began to plant kisses down the length of Matthew's body. He licked Matthew's nipples, first the right, then the left, until they pebbled, then licked his way down to his navel.

When he dipped his tongue in, Matthew giggled. "That tickles."

Lower still, Neil buried his nose in the tight curls around Matthew's cock, inhaling deeply. He smelled of spicy body wash and an underlying musk that was purely Matthew.

Neil licked around the flared head of Matthew's large cock. Sucking the head into his mouth, he stroked up and down the length as he tickled under the head with the tip of his tongue.

Matthew moaned as Neil moved to his smooth balls, taking each one into his mouth.

After a few moments, he lifted Matthew's legs, moving lower still and licking around his rim.

"Oh god," Matthew panted.

Neil continued to lick and tease as he reached for the lube. Pouring some onto his fingers, he circled Matthew's hole, then slid one digit in. He slowly moved in and out, sucking the head of Matthew's cock again.

"More, I need more," Matthew begged.

Neil added a second finger, scissoring them to open Matthew up.

"Ready. Now," Matthew said breathlessly.

Reaching for the condom, Neil rolled it down his hard length and applied some lube.

Neil lined up his dick and pushed, stopping once his cock-head was past the first ring of muscle.

"Okay?"

Matthew nodded, reaching up to pull Neil into a searing kiss.

Neil slowly pushed in, inch by inch until his balls were resting on Matthew's ass.

As they kissed again, Neil began to move, picking up speed as they found their rhythm together.

"Oh, yeah, right there," Matthew cried out. "Don't stop."

Neil wrapped his hand around Matthew's cock. It felt like hot steel in his grasp. At each upstroke, he moved his thumb along the underside, right at the frenulum, and Matthew shuddered.

"Don't stop," Matthew uttered once again. "Oh god, gonna come."

Neil felt Matthew's hot release on his hand and stomach.

As Matthew came, his ass tightened its grip around Neil's cock, and Neil felt his own orgasm take over.

"Ungh," he groaned, nearly blacking out. Kissing Matthew over and over, their breathing finally slowed.

Neil started to pull out, but Matthew stopped him, grabbing Neil's ass and pulling him back in.

"Stay right there for a minute, please," he said quietly. "Rest your full weight on me. Feels so good."

They kissed slowly and tenderly. Then kissed again. Neil smiled.

"I've fallen hard for you, you know." He kissed Matthew's nose.

"I guess it's a good thing that I've fallen for you too," Matthew whispered.

"I think we're gonna need more than a washcloth to clean this mess up." Neil slipped out of Matthew and removed the condom, tying it off. "Let's take a quick shower."

NEIL WOKE SUDDENLY, his bladder full. He tapped his phone on the nightstand and saw that it was only three twenty-seven. Resigned to the fact that he wouldn't sleep again until he relieved the pressure, he padded to the bathroom to pee. Hopefully, he'd be able to snuggle up to Matthew and fall back to sleep.

He returned to bed only to find it empty. The covers were cool to the touch on Matthew's side of the bed. It seemed he hadn't noticed he was alone when he first woke.

So where was Matthew? Had he decided to go back to his own cabin at some point? Everything had seemed fine between them last night.

Neil peered out into the living area. The moon cast a faint glow through the partially opened drapes across the sliding door, and he could see Matthew's silhouette on the sofa.

"Hey, sweetheart," he said quietly. "Are you all right?"

"Yeah," sighed Matthew. "Just thinking."

"Oh, I don't like the sound of that."

Matthew chuckled, but there was no humor in it.

"Sorry. Ben will be the first to tell you that Rob overthinks everything, but trust me, I'm the champ where overthinking is concerned."

"Care to tell me about it? I've been told I'm a pretty good listener."

Matthew patted the sofa cushion next to him, and Neil sat down.

"I guess I just keep waiting for the other shoe to drop," Matthew began.

"What do you mean?"

"Frankly, I've never fallen for a guy this quickly," Matthew confessed. "Not even Stephen. You almost seem too good to be true, and that scares me."

"I'll admit that I kinda feel the same. I've told you about a couple of the guys that I've gone out with recently, and trust me when I say, it's always been like that. I seem to attract the psychos and weirdos. But you're different. And yeah, that's kinda scary."

Matthew took Neil's hand.

"Remember when I told you about my breakup with Stephen? About how he told me that maybe I should end it all since I was such a big coward? Well, I seriously considered it. Ending it, I mean. I went so far as to actually buy some pills from someone. But I couldn't go through with it." He smiled wistfully. "I guess Stephen was right. I am a coward."

"Hey. Stop that right there. You're not a coward. Stephen was a jerk, and I'm sorry that he pushed you like that. The fact that you couldn't go through with it shows me that you're a strong and determined man. If you had succeeded in—god, I can't even say it—doing that …" Neil shook his head. "But you didn't. You didn't let him win. That makes you so fucking strong, sweetheart. Never forget that."

"Thanks. And you're right. I did see a therapist for a while after all of that, and I know deep down that I wasn't a coward, but when it was all happening, I felt like a failure. And some days, I guess I still feel broken." Matthew paused, trying to even out his breathing.

"I guess I let my brain get the better of me tonight. I woke up about an hour and a half ago, and everything just started spinning around in my head, and I couldn't stop it. I asked myself what I thought I was doing, getting involved with someone like you. That you deserve so much better than me. It just got out of control. Thanks for talking me off the ledge."

"No problem. And for the record, I don't think you're broken, and I keep thinking that you deserve someone better than me. So I guess we're even." Neil leaned over and gave Matthew a gentle kiss.

"Now how about we crawl our naked bodies back under the covers and see if we can get a bit more sleep? We've got a busy day ahead of us."

"Sounds like an ideal plan but only if we can cuddle."

"Oh, baby, I'm gonna cuddle the hell outta you."

CHAPTER 14

Sunday, October 16, Istanbul, Turkey

It was a busy day indeed. In fact, two busy days were in store for them.

Today, they were in Istanbul, and tomorrow they'd be in Kusadasi, and they had tours planned with their group for both days.

Matthew and Neil showered and dressed quickly—their middle-of-the-night chat had caused them to almost over-sleep—and joined most of their group for breakfast before heading out on a whirlwind tour of Istanbul, including the Blue Mosque, Hagia Sophia, the Turkish Bazaar, and a trip across the Bosphorus Strait.

"As beautiful as the Blue Mosque and Hagia Sophia are," Matthew told his friends as they reached the bus for their trip across the Bosphorus, "I'm really excited for this next part. Once we cross, we're still in Istanbul, but we're also in Asia."

"Really?" Julie said, amazed. "How did I miss that?"

"It's so cool, isn't it?" Matthew continued. "Not only am I in Europe for the first time, I also get to visit Asia!"

Their last stop before returning to the ship was a stop at the Grand Bazaar for some shopping. The bazaar was an interesting experience. The indoor venue consisted of several main "streets," with numerous side roads off them. It was very crowded, with vendors yelling over each other, trying to attract attention to their wares. Vendors were selling clothes, souvenirs, spices, brassware, and everything in between for as far as the eye could see. All in all, it was rather overwhelming, but they stuck together and kept to the main walkways as they perused the merchandise.

Matthew stopped to buy a box of Turkish delight candy, and at the same booth, Sam saw a brass coffee grinder that she once saw a TV chef use as a pepper mill, so she bought two—one for her and another for Rob and Ben.

Tracing their steps back out of the bazaar proved to be a bit challenging, but after several minutes, they were rewarded with gorgeous blue skies, bright sunshine, and fresh air.

"Whew!" Neil exclaimed. "That was fun, but I don't think I need to go there again." The rest of the group nodded in agreement.

<hr>

ONCE BACK ON THE SHIP, they all returned to their respective cabins to freshen up. They'd agreed to meet at the Trident Lounge for a relaxing drink after all the walking they had done on their tour.

Matthew and Neil were the first to arrive. They waved at

Marco, one of the bar waiters who had quickly become a favorite of the group, and sat at one of the available tables.

"Looks like a lot of passengers are still out in the city somewhere," Matthew said, scanning the nearly empty bar.

"Good afternoon, gentlemen." Marco approached them, smiling. "What can I get for you today?"

"Woodford Reserve on the rocks please, Marco," Matthew replied.

"I'll have the same," Neil added.

"Very good. Will any of the others be joining you?" Marco inquired.

"Yes," said Neil. "In fact, here's Sam now."

Sam sat down across from Matthew, a bit breathless. "Hi, Marco. May I have a cosmopolitan, please?"

"Of course, Miss Samantha. I'll be back in a moment with your drinks."

"So, boys," Sam addressed them both. "How are things going?"

Matthew smiled broadly. "Really good, Sam."

Sam looked relieved. "I'm happy to hear that."

She turned to Neil, a twinkle in her eye. "I'll only say this once, Neil. I know you're Kyle's best friend, but Matthew is like a brother to me. If you hurt him, they'll never find your body."

Neil looked shocked. "Um, no ... of course not. I ... um, would never deliberately do ... um, anything to hurt him," he stammered.

"Relax, sweetheart," Matthew said, taking Neil's hand. "She's teasing." He stared at Sam for a moment. "Well, sort of."

Sam laughed. "Yeah, relax, Neil. I wouldn't kill you. But I can make you squirm for a long time."

"Wow," Neil uttered nervously. "Kyle was right, you are scary."

"Hey, I just protect my own. You were already like family because of Kyle, but this"—she gestured between them—"just solidifies it more. Just don't fuck it up."

"Be nice," Matthew scolded. "We're both going into this with eyes wide open. We know it won't be easy to make a long-distance relationship work, but we agreed that we want to try."

"Okay, I'll behave," Sam agreed. "And please let me know if I can help out with travel arrangements for you. I've been known to work magic."

"Good to know."

Marco returned with their drinks just as Kyle and Jon reached the group. They pulled a nearby table closer and joined their friends.

After placing a drink order, Kyle asked, "So, what are you guys talking about?"

"Oh, nothing much." Matthew chuckled. "Sam just told Neil that if he hurts me, they'll never find his body."

"Shit," Jon said, shaking his head. "I got the same lecture from her, and I'm her cousin!"

"Yeah, she told me the same thing," Kyle moaned.

"What the hell, Sam," Matthew sputtered. "Do you give everyone that same speech?"

"Only those I care about, sweetie. And I do care about all of you. You're my family."

Marco discreetly placed drinks in front of Jon and Kyle.

"Now let's toast," Sam continued, raising her glass. "To love and family."

———

THE GROUP HAD DECIDED to have dinner together at Caspian's, the ship's Italian restaurant, and Matthew and Neil arrived a few minutes before their reservation. Sam and Julie were seated at the small bar near the entrance.

"Good evening, ladies." Matthew smiled as they approached the two women.

"Hi, guys," Julie replied, then sipped from her martini glass.

"We missed you for drinks this afternoon, Julie."

"I didn't sleep all that well last night, and after all the walking we did during the tour today, I just needed to crash for a couple of hours." Her eyes were bright behind the large green glasses she had on. They matched the lime-colored top she wore with off-white slacks.

Soon the rest of their party arrived, and they were seated for dinner. After choosing a selection of appetizers they could share, along with pasta and main courses, the conversation turned to tomorrow's shore excursion to Ephesus, a short distance from the port of Kuşadası, Turkey, where the ship would dock.

"I'm really looking forward to visiting the ancient city," Matthew told the group. "There are fragments of many of the ruins still in the city, including the Library of Celsus and the Temple of Hadrian. I'm hoping to get photos of some of the architectural details."

"What for, Matthew?" Julie was curious.

"Sometimes they inspire me with ideas for new jewelry designs. I took a few pottery classes in college and have been thinking about incorporating some smaller ceramic or porcelain designs into some pendants. I've learned that inspiration can strike at any time. Perhaps it will be tomorrow for me."

He paused to take a sip of his red wine.

"But even if it doesn't, I'm having a great time on the cruise, so absolutely no complaints from me." He placed his hand over Neil's, which was resting on the table.

"I think it's fascinating that you can see something like part of a ruin and that inspires you to design something completely different," Julie said, the awe clear in her voice. "My brain doesn't work that way at all."

"Trust me," Matthew continued, "it doesn't always work that way, but I've learned over the years to take photos or create sketches of things that I see. Even if it doesn't inspire me right away, looking back at them later can sometimes trigger an idea."

"Well, when it happens, please let me know." Julie looked pointedly at Matthew. "The thought of a piece of jewelry that combines pottery and metal and who knows what else that might come out of your head is very intriguing to me. I may need to get something."

"It's a deal, Julie."

Their waiter appeared with several appetizers, and their focus shifted to the assortment of food in front of them.

After dinner, several of their friends wanted to go to the ship's dance club, Change of Latitude. Julie in particular had gotten her second wind after napping that afternoon and wanted to dance the night away.

Matthew and Neil begged off.

"We're just going to take a leisurely stroll, maybe get a nightcap, and then head to bed," Matthew told them. "We've got another busy day tomorrow, and I, for one, don't wanna be draggin' my ass all day."

They parted ways, and after a short walk around the promenade on Deck 6, Matthew and Neil decided to skip the after-dinner drink and took an elevator back to Deck 12.

As they ambled down the hallway, Matthew turned to Neil, "Would you like to stay with me tonight?"

"Sure, although I gotta be honest, I really am beat." Matthew detected a blush in Neil's cheeks.

"Oh, yeah, I didn't mean to imply that we'd do much more than cuddle. I totally meant what I said when I told our friends that I wanted to be well rested tomorrow."

"I'd love to cuddle with you tonight, handsome."

Matthew wasn't sure what it was, but he always got a little giddy inside when Neil called him handsome. It made him feel warm all over, like he was someone special.

"I'll leave the sliders unlocked for you," Matthew said. Then giving Neil a quick peck on the lips, he went into his suite.

Once inside, he unlocked the door to the balcony, then quickly stripped and took a two-minute shower just to wash the day's sweat and grime off. Toweling off, he brushed his teeth and slipped on a pair of neon-blue trunks. He'd caught Neil checking out his ass once or twice, so why not wrap it up in something nice and bright?

As he finished filling out the breakfast-order card to hang

on the doorknob, he heard the sliders open and turned to see Neil enter the cabin, wearing only a pair of black boxer briefs.

"I know I said I was tired, but god, you look good enough to eat."

"Funny, I'm thinking the same thing." Neil's eyes scanned Matthew up and down, stopping on his crotch.

"C'mere," Matthew said huskily.

They hugged, kissing deeply.

Matthew felt Neil's hands grab his ass, kneading his cheeks. As they continued to kiss, Matthew could feel himself lengthening against Neil. He slipped his hands into the back of Neil's underwear, running his finger along Neil's crack.

Several moments passed. They touched, licked, and kissed until they were both straining again in their shorts.

"Okay," panted Neil. "I know we said we weren't gonna do anything, but there's no way I can go to sleep like this." He palmed his erection, the head of his cock poking out from the waistband of his boxers. "You know what I'd really like to do?"

"What?" asked Matthew, breathless.

"I wanna jerk you off and watch you come. Would that be okay?"

"Fuck yeah."

Neil reached over and dragged Matthew's trunks off, then pulled his own down. Grabbing Matthew's hand, he walked him to the bedroom.

Once Matthew was lying in the middle of the bed, Neil straddled him, positioning himself so that his cock was just below Matthew's.

Neil leaned forward for a kiss, then wrapped his hand around Matthew's dick, stroking it slowly.

"Mmmm," Matthew moaned quietly. "Feels so good."

Reaching for the bottle of lube Matthew had left on the nightstand, Neil dribbled some onto Matthew's cock, rubbing small circles with his thumb along the underside of the head.

Matthew grabbed the lube and coated his fingers, then slipped them under Neil's balls and traced around Neil's hole.

Bending once again to take Matthew's mouth in a searing kiss, Neil increased the speed of his strokes along Matthew's considerable length.

Matthew groaned into Neil's mouth, sucking on his tongue. Breaking the kiss, he panted, "Don't stop."

Neil leaned back and stared into Matthew's eyes. "Come for me, handsome."

As Matthew felt himself tumble over the edge, he pushed the tip of his finger into Neil's ass and watched the expression on Neil's face morph as he too climaxed.

Neil lay on Matthew's stomach, kissing him over and over again as their cum mingled between them.

"Wow, that was hot," Matthew finally said once he was able to catch his breath.

Neil got up and padded to the bathroom. Matthew could hear water running, and a few moments later, Neil returned with a warm, wet washcloth. After cleaning Matthew carefully, he tossed the cloth into the bathroom, then they snuggled under the covers.

CHAPTER 15

Monday, October 17, Kusadasi, Turkey

"Getting breakfast delivered this morning was such a good idea." Neil stepped out of the shower and handed a towel to Matthew.

"I thought it might save us some time this morning, seeing as we didn't get to sleep quite as early as we'd planned last night."

Neil felt himself blush. "Totally worth it, though."

Wrapping the towel around his waist, Neil went to the sliding doors at the balcony.

"I'll be back in a minute."

Entering his cabin, Neil paused for a moment. *Wow, last night was way hotter than I expected. What is it about Matthew that revs me up like that? Well, whatever it is, I hope it never stops!*

Clearing his head with a shake, he dressed quickly, then returned to Matthew's cabin carrying the towel.

"Are you ready to go?" he called out as he slipped through the sliding doors.

"Yeah." Matthew appeared in the bedroom doorway, pulling a purple polo shirt over his head and down across his stomach.

Neil swallowed, staring at Matthew's belly as it disappeared beneath the shirt.

"Um, wanna skip today's tour and um, just hang out here?" Neil stammered.

"We'll have plenty of time later to fool around, you horndog." Matthew chuckled as he pushed Neil toward the door, and they went off in search of the rest of their party.

***

Sam waved to them as they approached the Atlantis Theater.

"There you are. I thought maybe you both overslept this morning," she teased.

"Not at all. We decided to have breakfast delivered this morning so that we could sleep in a bit, that's all."

"Nice. Okay, now that everyone's here, we can get our stickers so that we're all on the same bus together."

They only had to wait about fifteen minutes until their group was called, and once on the bus, they sat as near to each other as they could, chatting about the tour and what they'd do afterward. Matthew seemed a bit quieter than usual, but Neil thought that perhaps he hadn't gotten enough sleep the night before, so he didn't mention anything.

Once they arrived at the ruins of the ancient city of Ephesus, they followed their tour guide, Hugo, as they entered through the Hercules Gate and walked down Curetes Street.

Their guide pointed out the remains of various shops and temples along the way, even stopping to show them an ancient public bathroom with a bench row of seats. This was where Ephesian men would begin their day gossiping with each other as they took care of business.

The street ended at the Celsus Library, where their group marveled at the ruins of the two-story facade and took lots of photos. Hugo explained that at one time, the library held over twelve thousand parchment scrolls in several different languages.

Next, they passed an ancient theater, which could hold twenty-five thousand people. History said that not only did St. Paul preach there at one time, but gladiators fought there during the Roman period. Their tour concluded as they exited the city on Arcadian Street.

"That was fascinating," Neil exclaimed as they strolled back to their bus.

"It certainly was," Matthew agreed. "I'm not really religious anymore, but to walk along the streets of a city that I remember hearing about as a kid in Bible study ..." He trailed off and shook his head. "I dunno, it's kinda surreal."

"It sure is," Sam added. "I'm really glad we decided to take this tour."

"Matthew," Julie spoke to him over her seat back once they were all on the bus. "I noticed that you had your sketchbook out a few times. Inspiration for more jewelry designs?"

"Yeah," Matthew admitted. "I do take a lot of photos, but every now and then I feel the urge to draw something. I can't really explain why, but over the years I've learned not to ignore it."

"Well, I think it's quite cool, Matthew," Ben remarked. "And I hope we'll get to see the results at some point."

It was still early when they got back on board, and there was a bit of chatter about what everyone was going to do next.

Neil noticed that even though Matthew had perked up while they were in Ephesus, he'd grown quiet again on the trip back to the ship.

"Are you okay, sweetheart?" he asked softly once they were in the elevator.

"Yeah, but I started with a headache this morning, and it's only gotten worse. I think I'm gonna go lie down for a little while."

"Do you get these headaches often?" Neil made the concern clear in his voice.

"Not really, but they do creep in every now and then. I've spoken to my doctor about it, and often they're stress related. I don't think that's the case now since I'm pretty relaxed on this trip, but hey, shit happens, right?"

Matthew didn't seem too concerned about it, so Neil wouldn't be either, but at that moment he realized how much he cared about Matthew.

"Okay, I'll stop hovering and let you rest."

They'd reached Matthew's cabin, and Neil followed him in.

"But please text or call if you need anything. I'll check in later, and maybe we can get dinner or something if you're feeling better."

"Yes, Mom," Matthew joked. "I'm sure I'll be fine after I nap for a couple of hours."

Neil gave him a chaste kiss on the lips and left.

Once in his own stateroom, he dropped off his backpack, washed his face, and brushed his teeth. Then he grabbed his phone and texted Kyle.

Hey. Where R U?

Tide Pool Bar, upstairs. Join us?

C U in a few.

Picking up his sunglasses, he was off in search of the bar and his friends.

It was sunny up on the pool deck, but Kyle and Jon had found a table in the shade on the starboard side of the ship. A bar waiter stopped at the table, and Neil ordered a drink.

"Where's Matthew?" Jon asked after the waiter departed. "You guys didn't have a fight or anything, did you?"

"No, nothing like that. He said he's had a headache all morning and just wanted to take a nap to see if that would help." Neil tried to keep the concern out of his voice but wasn't sure if he succeeded or not.

"I'm sure he'll be fine. So, things are going okay between the two of you?"

"Yeah, they are." Neil relaxed, thinking about how much he cared about Matthew. "He really is a great guy."

"Hmmm," Kyle murmured. "If I'm not mistaken, I hear a 'but' at the end of that."

"No, I ... um." Neil sighed. "I don't mean it like that. Matthew really is wonderful. We've talked about a lot of things: growing up, horror stories about some of our exes, things like that. We know we both have a bit of baggage, especially when it comes to never meeting the right guys in the past, and I think we really *get* each other. We seem to be compatible in many ways." Neil felt his face heat up and saw Kyle smile knowingly. "We like spending time together, and after some of the things he's told me, I think he's one of the strongest guys I've ever met."

"So what's the problem?" Kyle seemed confused. "He's great, you're great. You've obviously bumped uglies, and it seems that's okay." At Neil's glare, he added, "Hey, don't look at me like that. I know you, Neil, and it's all over your face that you've enjoyed some time in the sack together."

Neil shook his head and smiled. "You do know me well, don't you?"

"But if everything is good, I'm not sure why you sound hesitant."

"First of all, you know my luck with guys really sucks. How long will it take before Matthew realizes I'm not worth the effort?"

"I call bullshit. Of course you're worth the effort!" Kyle sounded exasperated. "You know I hate it when you put yourself down like that. You just said that you've talked, and you know that each of you has some baggage. I don't know Matthew's story, but I do remember Rob saying that his last boyfriend was a real dick. I say you both need to get over the past and move forward. Preferably together."

Neil smiled sheepishly but went on. "Secondly, and frankly, this is what's mostly on my mind, we live several hundred miles away from each other. How exactly are we gonna make this work?"

"Oh my god, Neil. Seriously?" Jon looked flabbergasted. "You know who you're talking to, right?"

"Yeah, seriously, Neil," Kyle chimed in. "Jon and I managed to make a long-distance relationship work pretty well, I think. And if that's not enough, what about my dad and Rob? They made a cross-country relationship work for almost two years before they decided to tie the knot."

"Think about it, Neil. There's inspiration for you and Matthew all around. You know we'll help in any way we can."

"Yeah, I get it." Neil was truly touched by the support he had from his found family. "And I really appreciate it. But don't forget, while I do have a bit of savings, I can't afford to be flying up to Massachusetts to see Matthew every weekend like your dad or Rob could."

"Granted, but it's still not a problem. Jon and I found a whole new appreciation for FaceTime. You'd be surprised how creative you can get." Kyle practically leered at him while Jon had the decency to lower his head as he blushed.

"Plus, you have a secret weapon." Jon looked a bit devious. "Sam is downright spooky when it comes to finding travel deals. With a little bit of planning, I'm sure she can save you a bunch of money."

Kyle quickly followed up. "And Rob and my dad would be more than happy to help out with such a worthy cause. I know for a fact that combined, they literally have millions of frequent flyer miles they'd be thrilled to donate."

"All right, all right, I surrender." Neil lifted his hands. "Really, thanks, you guys. I truly appreciate all your support."

"Hey, we've got you. After all, you're family, and we take care of our own."

NEIL WAS MEANDERING along Seaside Cove feeling a bit restless. After he'd chatted with Kyle and Jon for a bit longer, they'd decided to go back to their cabin for a brief nap before dinner. He'd picked up his phone several times to text Matthew but then decided against it. If Matthew had managed to fall asleep, he didn't want to disturb him. He was just passing the Trident Lounge when he saw Rob and Ben, hand in hand, approaching him.

"Hey, Neil," Rob said, smiling. "How are you doing?"

"Good, thanks. How are you guys?"

"Just great, thanks. We're just in search of a drink. Would you like to join us?"

"Thanks, but I don't want to intrude."

"Nonsense, you're not intruding. Join us, please." Ben walked to the end of the mostly empty bar and sat down.

As the bartender approached, Ben greeted him by name. "Hi, Marco. How are you doing today?"

"Fine, thank you. How are you and Sir Rob this fine day? And you too, Sir Neil."

Neil marveled that not only did Marco remember all their names but that he insisted on prefacing them with Sir for the guys and Miss or Lady for the women.

"We're all doing well but desperately in need of a beverage," Ben joked. "Can you help us out?"

"Of course. A double Woodford Reserve on the rocks for you, Sir Ben?"

"Yes, please."

"I'll have the same," said Rob.

"Let's keep it easy, then. I'll have one as well," echoed Neil.

"I don't mean to pry," Rob began once Marco had left to prepare their drinks, "but is there a reason Matthew's not with you?"

"Nothing sinister, I assure you. When we got back from the tour, he said he'd had a headache most of the day and wanted to lie down for a while. I admit I was a little concerned at first, but he assured me it's nothing to worry about." Neil couldn't keep the concern out of his voice.

"I know that he's had some issues with headaches in the past, so I'm sure he's got it under control." Rob looked sympathetic. "So I'm gonna guess this means that you two are getting a bit more serious, 'cause you clearly seem troubled by all of this."

Neil chuckled. "Yes to both. It seems we've connected very strongly. I've never really experienced anything like this before. And we both decided that we want to give it a try." Neil paused to sip his bourbon. "I do believe I'm falling in love with him. It seems a bit quick to me, but it's never been like this for me, so I'm not really sure what the hell is happening right now."

Ben smiled broadly. "Hey, don't let anyone tell you it's too soon, or you couldn't possibly know yet, or any other bullshit like that. It happens when it happens."

"Yeah, people have been known to fly thousands of miles just to say those three words." Rob looked tenderly at Ben. The love between them was palpable.

"I sense a story there." Neil was thoughtful. "And thank

you both for your support with this. I just don't want to fuck it up."

"Don't wait to tell him how you feel," Ben said somberly. "And if there's anything we can do to help, please let us know."

They toasted and drank.

Just then, Neil's phone buzzed.

"It's Matthew," he told them, looking up from his screen. "He's feeling better. He's gonna take a quick shower, then plans on coming to look for me."

"Tell him to join us here," Rob said. "Um, unless you'd rather be alone."

"Not at all." Neil smiled. "After all, Kyle and Jon reminded me earlier that we're family, and family sticks together."

Ben caught Marco's attention and ordered another round.

THEY'D RETURNED FROM DINNER, and Matthew had agreed to spend the night in Neil's bed. They were snuggling after reading for a little while.

Neil pulled Matthew closer and kissed the back of his neck.

"There's something I wanted to tell you, Matthew."

"Of course. Is everything okay?"

"Yeah, it's just that I got really worried earlier when you said you had a headache and wanted to lie down. I felt a bit helpless; I really wanted to make sure you were okay."

"It's fine. I was pretty confident that a nap would do the trick, and the fact that you were concerned about me feels really good. That's not something I'm especially used to."

"Well, it goes a bit beyond that." Neil took a breath. "The truth is, I love you, Matthew. I've never felt this way about anyone before."

Matthew turned and kissed Neil. "I love you too," he admitted. "I've just been too scared to say anything. I thought it was too soon or something."

Neil chuckled. "That's funny, I thought exactly the same thing. But when I was chatting with Ben and Rob earlier, Ben said, 'Don't let anyone tell you it's too soon.' He's right. When it's right, it's right."

They kissed again and again, but just as it started to heat up, Matthew yawned.

"Sorry, it's not the company, I promise."

"No worries. You need your rest."

With one final kiss, they drifted off to sleep in each other's arms.

CHAPTER 16

"Something's changed between the two of you," Sam announced as she sat near Matthew. They were having breakfast together before their tour of Athens.

"I have no idea what you're talking about." Matthew sipped his coffee innocently.

"Bullshit."

Neil chuckled. "Well, it might be that we finally admitted our true feelings last night. We love each other."

"About fucking time." Sam nodded knowingly. "Did I ever tell you how Ben flew all the way to Florida from California right after the cruise where he and Rob met, just so that he could tell Rob that he loved him?"

"Oh." Neil snickered. "So that's what happened."

Ben and Rob were sitting at the other end of the table. Ben shook his head and sighed. "I'm never gonna live that down, am I?"

"It was so totally romantic, sweetheart." Rob reached for Ben's hand. "There's nothing to live down. I loved it. And I love you."

They kissed, and the table sighed collectively.

"Not to change the subject," Ben injected. "What are you guys doing today?"

"We're taking a half-day tour in Athens," Mike Jr. said. "Mom and Dad are staying on the ship, so they offered to watch Wyatt while Becky and I go with the rest of the group."

"Yeah, it's Mike Jr. and Becky, Julie and me, Kyle and Jon, and Matthew and Neil," Sam told them. "After a short driving tour to see some of the sights, we visit the Acropolis, then have some time to shop and eat in the area they call the Plaka."

"What are you guys doing, Dad?" Kyle asked Ben and Rob.

"We're staying on the ship. We talked about maybe visiting the spa, and then we'll probably have lunch with Mike, Ellen, and Wyatt."

"Did anyone have plans for dinner tonight?" Rob asked the group. "Ben and I will ask Stewart to put something together for us if you'd like."

"That would be great." Matthew looked around the table and saw everyone nodding.

"Okay. Consider it done. Check the app on your phone later, and you should see the details. Enjoy your day in Athens."

Ben and Rob left the restaurant, and the others soon followed. Matthew had forgotten his backpack, so he went back to his cabin to grab it.

THE ACROPOLIS WAS SPECTACULAR. Matthew couldn't get over the fact that this ruin existed in the middle of Athens. The Parthenon was magnificent, with it's massive stone columns, and the nearby temple of Erechtheion, supported by the caryatids, was amazing. They all took lots of photos, including quite a few selfies.

When they reached the Plaka area, their tour guide said they had about two hours there for shopping and lunch before the bus would take them back to the ship. They also had the option to spend the rest of the afternoon in Athens and find their own transportation back to the pier. Sam shocked everyone in the group by saying that she wasn't interested in shopping and would prefer to find a nice place to eat and relax.

They strolled around a bit and found a little restaurant on a side street that had a nice outdoor dining area on the side of the building. They secured a table and were soon feasting on spanakopita, dolmades, and a traditional salad of cucumbers, tomatoes, green peppers, and red onions along with Kalamata olives and large planks of feta cheese. It was accompanied by local wine and beer.

"This was a great idea, Sam." Matthew sipped his wine. "Don't get me wrong, I love sightseeing, but sitting here with you all, partaking of some local food and drink, well, it doesn't get much better than this."

"Exactly," agreed Neil.

Eventually, they settled their bill and found their way back to the meeting spot for their tour. Mike Jr. and Becky decided to spend a little more time in the city and said they'd get a taxi back to the ship later. The rest of their group boarded the bus and waited for it to depart.

"What's everyone gonna do when we get back on the ship?" Kyle asked the group.

"The sun is shining, so I may lie out by the pool for a bit," Sam replied.

"I think I may want to catch a quick nap," Matthew said. "I'm not used to drinking at lunch."

"That sounds like a good idea," agreed Neil.

"Actually, a nap does sound nice," Jon admitted, grinning.

"Okay, text us later, and we can meet up before dinner," Kyle said. "Looks like I'll be napping for a little while too."

***

"So, do you want to nap with me?" Matthew asked Neil as they walked to their cabin.

"Sure. I'll never skip a chance to cuddle."

"Oh my god, you two are too cute." Kyle grinned at them. "And if you're still tired before dinner, we'll know that you did something other than nap."

"Who says we can't do both?" Neil asked innocently. They all laughed.

Once in Matthew's stateroom, they stripped to their underwear and got under the covers. Matthew set an alarm on his phone, then turned to Neil.

"Okay, we've got a couple of hours for a nap, and we'll still have plenty of time to shower and do other things before we meet them." He kissed Neil deeply.

They made out for a few minutes, and before too long, Matthew's hands were shoved down the back of Neil's trunks, cupping his ass. Eventually breaking the kiss, Matthew sighed.

"As much as I'd love to continue along this line, if we don't stop now, we'll never get that nap." And with that, he turned over to become the little spoon. He snuggled up against Neil, feeling his erection nestle into the crack of his ass.

Slowly, they drifted off to sleep.

MATTHEW WOKE to the alarm on his phone buzzing. As he switched it off, he felt Neil's arms tighten around him and a gentle kiss on his neck.

"I can't believe it's been two hours already." Matthew snuggled up against Neil. "I feel like I just closed my eyes."

"I know. But we probably should get up. We'll feel better after we shower, and then we can text Kyle and Jon." Neil made no move to get out of bed. Instead, he gripped Matthew even harder.

Matthew flipped over so that he was facing Neil. They kissed, and Matthew felt Neil's tongue slide along his lips. He opened up to him and felt Neil's tongue skim along the roof of his mouth.

"Mmmm," he moaned, sucking on Neil's tongue.

Pushing Neil onto his back, he slid down Neil's body, nipping and licking at his nipples until they peaked.

Matthew's hand moved south, and he gripped Neil's hard cock through the fabric. "Want to taste this," he panted between kisses along Neil's belly.

Neil lifted his ass from the bed, and Matthew pulled the trunks down. Neil's dick slapped his hairy belly, and he moaned. Matthew kissed the head of Neil's cock, then licked under the crown, causing yet another moan to escape. He licked up and down Neil's length, then tickled the underside with the tip of his tongue.

Matthew coated the middle finger of his left hand with saliva, then moved his hand under Neil's balls. Tapping his fingertip against Neil's hole, Matthew swallowed his cock as he stroked himself with his right hand.

Neil lightly gripped the sides of Matthew's head and spread his legs apart in invitation. Matthew eased his finger into Neil as he continued to suck.

"Oh yeah," Neil whispered. "So close."

Matthew's fingertip tapped Neil's prostate, and he heard Neil's grunt as he came. His hot seed hit the back of Matthew's throat, and he swallowed greedily, not wanting to miss a single drop. He felt his own orgasm rising, and he stroked himself until his release hit Neil's leg.

Neil pulled him up and kissed him hard.

"I love tasting myself on your tongue," Neil said huskily. His thumb swiped along Matthew's cock, collecting the cum on the tip and sucking it into his mouth.

"So hot," Matthew sighed, kissing Neil again.

Eventually, they climbed into the shower and managed to wash each other off without getting too distracted.

As they dressed, Matthew noticed a text from Jon saying he and Kyle were going to the pub for a drink and that Matthew and Neil should join them if they weren't, in Jon's words, "otherwise engaged."

"He's such a funny guy." Neil groaned. "Let's go. We might as well get the teasing over with."

As they sauntered down the promenade toward the Mermaid's Tail, Matthew spotted Kyle and Jon sitting at a table outside of the bar.

Once seated, they placed a drink order with a passing waiter.

"So how was the nap?" Jon asked, smirking.

"It was actually quite nice. We slept for about two hours." Matthew paused, checking to see if anyone could overhear them. He lowered his voice. "I'm not saying we didn't do other things after the nap, but the nap was really nice."

"Sweet," Kyle said, blushing slightly. "It sounds like we *all* had a good time. Especially after the nap."

They all chuckled. Matthew felt warm inside, knowing he could be himself with these guys. It was so nice not to have to hide anything from friends and be totally accepted for who you are. Their waiter returned with drinks. Matthew picked up his glass and said, "To naps. And the things that happen after naps."

They raised their glasses. "Cheers!"

"Hmm, I don't see anything in the app about dinner tonight. Didn't my dad say he'd arrange for something?" Kyle asked.

"He did, and I've worked up an appetite for sure," Matthew joked.

"I'm gonna text him to see what's going on," Kyle addressed the group.

"I wouldn't mind going to Kaiyo again for some teppanya-ki," Neil said.

"Dad hasn't made arrangements yet but said that Mike and Ellen are having dinner with Mike Jr., Becky, and Wyatt. He's gonna reach out to Stewart to see if he can get us a table for eight at Kaiyo. He'll send out a group text once he hears back."

"Sam and Julie are at the Trident Lounge. Marco's working, and they both really wanted cosmos," Jon said, looking at his phone. "Sam says we should join them."

"Sure," Kyle replied. "Tell her we'll be there once we finish our drinks."

CHAPTER 17

"Dinner was so much fun last night," Neil said over breakfast. He and Matthew were sitting with Kyle and Jon in the Bluefin Bistro.

They'd had the same chef as the last time they'd dined at Kaiyo, and even though the jokes were just as corny, they all laughed that much harder.

"I can't believe the cruise is almost over." Kyle shook his head and sipped his coffee. "It's all gone by way too quickly."

"I know," Matthew agreed. He placed his hand over Neil's, then smiled sadly. "I really don't want this to end."

"Hey, the vacation is ending, but we're not." Neil stared at Matthew. "We both want this. We're gonna make it work."

"I know, but I still don't want this cruise to end. I've been having too much fun."

"What time are we supposed to meet Sam and Julie at the

spa?" Jon checked his watch. They'd all decided to visit the Sanctuary thermal suite again that day.

"Not until ten o'clock, sweetheart," answered Kyle. "We've got plenty of time."

They lingered over breakfast and eventually made their way down to the spa. At the front desk, they found Sam and Julie along with Mike, Mike Jr., and Becky.

"Mom offered to watch Wyatt this morning so that we could experience the Sanctuary," Mike Jr. explained to the group. "That's not a problem, is it?"

"Of course not," Kyle told them. "The more the merrier."

After about an hour and a half of relaxation in the spa, they parted ways. Sam, Julie, and Becky wanted to check out the shops one more time while Kyle, Jon, and Mike Jr. headed to the pub for a drink. Kyle had told them that he and his cousin hadn't spent that much time together, so they were planning on catching up.

Neil and Matthew begged off joining them. "We want to spend some time together—just the two of us if that's okay."

"Of course," Jon assured them. "If you want to meet up later, text us."

They wandered around the ship for a while, with no destination in mind. Soon they were riding the elevator up to Deck 12 and their cabins. It was sunny but breezy, so they donned light jackets and met on their balcony with their Kindles in hand.

"I thought we could move two loungers together and sit for a while." Neil began to drag one of the lounge chairs over.

"That's a great idea. I must admit, as much as I've loved everything we've done on this cruise, I miss my quiet time."

"What do you mean?" Neil asked.

"When I get home from work, I usually pour myself a glass of wine and sit on my deck. I've got a great view of the Westport River. I just love watching the scenery around me and relaxing for about an hour. Helps settle me after a day at work."

"That sounds nice. I'd love to see that view sometime."

"Definitely. Speaking of which, do you have any more vacation time this year?"

"A few days that I'm going to use at Christmas. I'm gonna visit my family in Virginia," Neil said.

"Oh, then maybe you could come visit me in the spring?" Matthew sounded hopeful.

"I'd like that a lot. But let's go back to Christmas for a moment ..." Neil hesitated, then pushed on. "Are you able to take some time away from the shop? I was thinking you could come down to DC and maybe spend Christmas with me and my family?"

"Seriously? You want me to spend Christmas with your family? I'd love to."

Neil beamed. "Excellent. How much time can you take off? If I remember correctly, Christmas is on a Sunday. I was planning on driving to my mom's on Saturday. I've got to be back to work on Wednesday, but if you could stay for a few more days, we could spend New Year's together too."

"Let me check with Christine; she's the store manager. Her family is local, so she normally doesn't travel anywhere at Christmastime. And it's off-season, so the store's not overly busy. I'm pretty sure I can take a week or so off to visit you."

"Oh, that's perfect. I haven't talked to Kyle yet about what he and Jon are doing for the holidays, but if they're around, maybe we can plan to ring in the New Year with them."

"This is gonna be so much fun. I haven't spent Christmas with my family for a few years now," Matthew admitted. "I usually get together with friends like Sam or Rob and Ben. And while that's always been a good time, something tells me this Christmas is gonna be extra special."

THEY ENDED up ordering a light lunch from room service and spent some time reading and dozing in the sun. Just before five, both of their phones buzzed.

"It's a text from Ben," Neil said. "He's inviting everyone to dinner at the Seahorse Steakhouse tonight at eight thirty. Seems like he's even made arrangements for someone from the children's program to babysit Wyatt so that Mike Jr. and Becky can join us."

"That's great. I think I'll text Kyle and see if he and Jon want to meet us for drinks around six thirty."

"Perfect. I'll text Sam too. Let's try to meet at the Trident Lounge."

"SAM, did you buy anything else when you went shopping earlier?" Neil and Matthew were sitting with Sam and Julie, enjoying cocktails while they waited for Kyle and Jon to arrive.

"Yes, as a matter of fact. I'd been eyeing a dress in one of the shops and decided to treat myself. And I talked Julie into buying a bag and a scarf."

"That's great."

"And what did you gentlemen do this afternoon?" Sam sipped her cosmo.

"We sat out on the balcony and read for a while. We also made plans to spend Christmas together."

"Oh, nice. Who's going where?"

"I'll go to DC and then spend Christmas with Neil and his family in Virginia," Matthew told her.

"Excellent. Once you know your travel days, let me know. I'll start looking for some options for you. There aren't a lot of deals around the holidays, but if there's one to be had, I'll find it."

"Thanks, Sam."

"OH MY GOD, I definitely ate too much," Neil groaned.

"I think we all did," Jon agreed.

Dinner had been superb. They'd feasted on shrimp cocktail, beef carpaccio, and oysters for appetizers, followed by filets, rib eyes, and lobsters for main courses. Finally, their waiter had encouraged them to share a couple of desserts. Neil had to admit, the key lime pie had been excellent.

"I think I need to walk some of this off before I turn in. Ben, Rob, thank you again for a wonderful time." Neil stood and held his hand out to Matthew. They bid everyone good night and left the dining room.

They walked along Seaside Cove until they reached the elevators, which they took up to the pool deck. There were glass barriers that helped reduce the wind on deck, so they took their time and strolled leisurely around the deck, enjoying the moon and stars in the velvet sky.

"Looking back, I can't believe I almost didn't come on this cruise," Neil said. "Kyle had to talk me into it. And I still wasn't sure."

"I know exactly what you mean. The day I got the invitation, Sam called and pretty much guilted me into coming. And of course, Christine was relentless."

"I'm glad our friends know us better than we know ourselves."

"Amen to that," Matthew concurred. "I'm so glad I met you, Neil. I know it's only been a couple of weeks. But I can't imagine my life without you now."

"I know what you mean." They stopped in a secluded corner, and Neil kissed Matthew tenderly.

Breaking the kiss, Neil yawned. "Sorry, it's not you."

"I understand; I'm beat too. Let's go to bed."

CHAPTER 18

Thursday, October 20, Venice, Italy

"Good morning, sunshine." Matthew felt quite chipper today. They would be in Venice but weren't scheduled to arrive until lunchtime, so they decided to sleep in this morning. "I ordered room service for breakfast. It should be here shortly."

"Sounds good." Neil got up, kissed Matthew, then stumbled into the bathroom. In their short time together, Matthew had learned that Neil wasn't really a morning person.

When Neil returned, he was wearing one of the robes that the cruise line provided in their suites. Just then, the doorbell rang, and Matthew answered it. A waiter wheeled a cart into the room and placed their breakfast on the dining table. Matthew handed him a tip, and the waiter departed with a smile, saying, "Enjoy, gentlemen."

There was fruit and yogurt, orange juice and coffee, and of course, English muffins with peanut butter.

"This is perfect. Thanks, Matthew." Neil smiled and took a sip of his coffee.

THEY WAITED at a water-taxi stand with their tour guide. It was just Neil and Matthew, Kyle and Jon, and Sam. The others had chosen different excursions, but they were heading to the island of Murano to see how their world-famous glass was made. After that, they'd visit one of the many churches in Venice, and finally, they'd ride a gondola through part of the city. When they had discussed things to do, that had sounded like the most bang for their buck.

They all agreed that the glassmaking was fascinating, and Matthew bought a small glass dish in the gift shop. Sam found a pair of earrings with a matching pendant that she hemmed and hawed about until Matthew convinced her that she'd regret it if she left without them.

The church was, well, a church. Yes, there were some interesting architectural details, but not being an overly religious group of friends, they were just a bit "churched out." It seemed that churches were a big attraction in many European countries, but they'd all had their fill at that point.

They finally arrived at the gondolas near the train station, and Neil apparently couldn't contain himself.

"Oh my god, I never in my life thought I'd actually get to ride in a gondola. This is so exciting!"

Matthew smiled at him, feeling some of Neil's excitement rub off on him.

"I know, right? This is gonna be really cool."

Their guide had explained that the gondolier would tell

them where to sit and not to argue. "He must be careful with the weight distribution so that the gondola stays balanced. Just sit where he tells you."

Once seated, the gondolier pushed off, and their heads swiveled in unison as they took in all the scenery. They traveled along some of the smaller canals, and Matthew took photo after photo of their surroundings.

"This is all so beautiful," Kyle said, clearly in awe. "Although I must say, I didn't expect the canals to be this dirty." Looking around, Matthew could see empty water bottles and plastic wrappers floating in the water.

"Yeah, it's sad, really," he said. "All of this beauty around us, and it's being spoiled by inconsiderate people."

When their ride finally ended, Sam pulled out a map that she got from the tour guide and tried to figure out where they were.

"Ah," she said, pointing to a spot on the map. "We're here. The Rialto Bridge isn't too far if you want to see that."

As they turned to follow Sam, Matthew's phone buzzed with an incoming call.

Matthew answered, "Hey, Marcus, what's up? … Oh no. Is he okay? … Tomorrow, why? … Huh, why … what's going on? … Okay. I'll talk to you later … Thanks, Marc. Love you."

Neil had stepped closer to Matthew. "What's wrong?"

"That was my brother, Marcus. It seems my dad's been taken to the hospital. They're pretty sure he had a heart attack."

"Oh no." Matthew could hear the concern in Neil's voice. "What can I do to help?"

Matthew noticed that Sam had moved off to the side and

was on the phone. She saw him staring at her and ended the call.

"Matthew, I hope you don't mind, but I called Rob. He and Ben are sorry about your dad. Do you want to try and catch an earlier flight home? I can check on schedules for you if you'd like."

"No, it's fine. Marcus said he's stable, and they think the worst is over for now anyway." He shook his head. "But Marcus said that Dad's been asking for me. I don't understand why. He's not really wanted to talk to me in years except to tell me that I'm an abomination. Why is he asking for me?"

"I guess you'll have to talk to him to find out," Neil said quietly. "What do you want to do now?"

"I'm not really in the mood for any more sightseeing. I think I'll just go back to the ship. But you guys go on ahead and enjoy yourselves."

"I'll go back with you," Neil said immediately. "And don't argue with me. I'm not leaving you alone right now."

Matthew smiled sadly. "Thank you, sweetheart."

"Call me if you decide to try and leave earlier," Sam told him. "I can't promise there are many options, but I'll do what I can."

"Thanks, Sam. I appreciate it."

Sam consulted the map again and directed them on the quickest way back to the ship.

"I'M SORRY, Neil. I know I'm not the best company right now, but I'm feeling all out of sorts." They had returned to the ship and were making their way to the closest elevators.

"No need to apologize, sweetheart. I can't begin to imagine what you're feeling right now. Is there anything I can do to help you?"

"I think I want to just hang out in my cabin," Matthew started. "And frankly, I could use a drink. But I guess I don't really want to be alone. Would you stay with me?"

"You couldn't get rid of me if you tried. How about we stop at the Trident Lounge and grab drinks. We can take them back to your suite and just relax there."

"That sounds perfect. I think I'd like some bourbon on the rocks."

When they reached the bar, Neil ordered two Woodford Reserve doubles on the rocks. Once they were in Matthew's cabin, he told his lover to sit on the sofa, and he carefully removed Matthew's shoes, resting his feet on the coffee table.

"What else do you need?"

"Just you beside me." Matthew patted the cushion next to him.

Neil sat close and took his hand. They quietly sipped their drinks.

"I feel so conflicted," Matthew finally uttered. "I'm scared for Dad, of course. Even though we haven't had the best relationship for the past few years, he's still my dad, and I love him. I want him to be okay."

"Of course, you do," Neil murmured. "You're a good son despite the troubles you two have had in the past."

"But I'm not sure why Dad has been asking for me. I can't imagine he just wants to berate me some more. He should be focused on getting better."

"I don't know, love. But I'm sure you can find out when

you talk to him. Did Marcus say anything about him being able to talk on the phone? Maybe you could call him?"

"It didn't sound like it. Marcus said they were going to run some tests and that Dad was sleeping a lot. I don't want to disturb him if he needs his rest."

"Okay." Neil paused, and Matthew sensed he wanted to say more.

"What?" Matthew turned to Neil and smiled. "I can almost see the wheels turning. What's on your mind?"

"Well, I was wondering if you've thought about what you're gonna do when you get home tomorrow?"

"I actually did think about that while we were walking back to the ship. I think I'd like to drive up to Nashua as soon as we land in Boston. It will only take about an hour to drive there from the airport."

"Okay. I can ask Sam if she can arrange a rental car for you if you'd like."

"Yeah," Matthew said, "that's a good idea."

"Um, one more thing, though," Neil said softly. "Would it be okay if I came with you?"

"You don't have to do that, sweetheart. I know you've got to get back to DC."

"I know I don't have to, but I'd really like to. If it's okay, I mean. I, um … well, I don't want to intrude on your family. I know it's a really stressful time, but on the other hand, I don't want you to be alone right now. I especially don't want you to drive up to Nashua alone."

Matthew squeezed Neil's hand. "How the hell did I get so lucky? I think you're a little crazy to want to put yourself in the middle of my family drama, but I'd love to have the company. And honestly, even though I know my brothers have my back, I really would prefer not to face my parents alone."

"Okay, it's settled. We're doing this together."

SAM MADE the arrangements for a rental car for them in Boston. Shortly after she texted them both with all the details, Matthew and Neil each got a text from Rob asking if Matthew was up for a short visit.

Sure. Come on over.

A few minutes later, there was a knock at the door. Neil went to answer it.

"Hey, Matthew." Rob entered with Kyle at his side.

"Hi, guys."

"You may have heard that I can sometimes be a bit of a control freak," Rob began, chuckling. "So we've come up with an idea on how to make this a bit easier on you tomorrow."

"Okay," Neil replied.

Matthew shook his head. "What have you done now, Rob?"

"Hey, it's really good. So, when you pack your stuff tonight, make sure you have a couple of changes of clothes in your carry-on. When we land in Boston tomorrow, we'll take your checked luggage. That way you don't have to worry about it. Matthew, you can get your bag from us when you get back to Westport."

"And Neil, Jon and I will take charge of your bag," Kyle added. "I know you're scheduled on a flight from Providence with Jon and me on Sunday, but if you need to change that, we can take your bag back to DC, and I'll just bring it to your apartment."

"And if you do need to change your flights," Rob picked up the conversation, "call Sam, and she'll make all the arrangements."

"If you're not gonna be back to the office by Monday, I can talk to your manager if you want me to. I'm sure he'll understand and won't give you any shit about it."

"Thanks, guys," Matthew and Neil said in unison.

"We're both so lucky to have you all on our side," Matthew added.

"Hey," Rob said, his voice shaking a bit, "don't forget, we're family. And we take care of each other."

CHAPTER 19

It was early evening when Neil pulled into the parking lot at the Southern New Hampshire Medical Center and found a parking spot.

Their entire group had held a tearful goodbye at the airport almost two hours earlier. Neil and Matthew had promised to keep everyone in the loop, then went to pick up their rental car. They had encountered some traffic leaving the city but had finally arrived.

"I texted Marcus and told him that you are coming with me, and I told him you are my boyfriend; I hope that was okay?"

"Of course, sweetheart. We hadn't really said it yet, but I guess we are boyfriends. And I have to tell you, I really like the sound of that." Neil smiled.

"Me too," Matthew said shyly. "I know Marcus and Micah

will be okay with it, but I plan to play it by ear with my folks. I don't want to upset my dad at this point."

"That's fine. I'll follow your lead."

As they exited the elevator, Neil saw a woman and two men standing near the nurses' station. He pointed, and Matthew looked over. One of the men saw them and hurried over, giving Matthew a hug.

"Hey, Micah," Matthew hugged him back. "This is my boyfriend, Neil."

"Hey, Micah, nice to meet you." They shook hands.

The woman and other man walked over to them, and Matthew hugged both of them.

Not wanting to open a can of worms with his mom right then, he decided not to use the word boyfriend for her introduction. "Mom, Marcus, this is my friend Neil. He offered to come with me as he didn't think I should be alone on the drive up here."

"Hi, I'm Marcus. Nice to meet you, Neil." He smiled, and they shook hands.

"I'm Viola. It's very nice to meet you, Neil. And thank you for looking out for my son."

"It's a pleasure, ma'am," Neil said, shaking her proffered hand.

"How's Dad doing? Can I see him?" Matthew asked, hope clearly written on his face.

"Sure, baby. Let's go talk to the nurse. His doctor had gone in to check on him; that's why we were out here waiting." Viola led Matthew to the nurses' station.

Neil turned to Marcus. "Is your dad doing okay? Matthew's been really worried since you called him yesterday."

"Yeah, pretty much. They're still running some tests, but they said he should be fine. Just might need to slow down a bit." He looked closely at Neil. "You really care about Matthew, don't you?"

"Yeah, I do." Neil admitted. "I haven't known him for all that long, but he's very special to me. I'll do whatever I can to help him."

"I can see it when you look at him. I'll be honest with you; Micah and I will support Matthew completely. We only want him to be happy. Mama seems to be on the fence about things and doesn't really say much. Even more so lately. But Dad's a tough nut to crack. Although I have to admit, he's seemed a bit different the last couple of times I've talked to him." He paused, watching Viola put her arm around Matthew and lead him down the hall toward their dad's room.

"Not sure what it is, but it's almost like he's mellowed a little. I wanted to talk to Mama about it, but then this happened, and I haven't had the chance. Maybe it's a good sign. I just don't know."

"Thanks for telling me. But no matter what your dad says to him, I'm not going anywhere. I love Matthew, and I want to be part of his life."

MATTHEW STEPPED into his dad's hospital room and stared at the man lying in the bed. It looked as if his dad had aged ten years.

Viola stayed near the door, gently pushing Matthew forward.

"Hey, Dad." Matthew reached the side of the bed and saw his dad open his eyes.

"Matty, is that really you?" Matthew smiled at the nickname his dad had called him as a child. He'd not heard it for many years.

"Yeah, Dad, I'm here. Got here as fast as I could. How are you doin'?"

"I'm still here, right? Gonna take more than a little heart attack to get rid of me."

"I was so scared when Marcus called me. And when he said you were asking for me, I feared the worst. Dad ... are you really gonna be okay?"

"Sure. Ask your Mama. They're running all these tests 'cause that's what they do. But everything they've told us so far is that I'm gonna be just fine. This was just a little scare to get me to slow down." He chuckled.

Matthew turned to Viola, and she nodded. Matthew relaxed at her confirmation that his dad would be okay.

"Okay, that makes me feel so much better, Dad. I'm really glad I came to see you; it's been way too long."

"That it has, son. And that's what I wanted to talk to you about. When this all happened, I thought maybe I was a goner, and I wouldn't get the chance to talk to you. That's why I kept asking for you, Matty." His dad paused for a moment and closed his eyes.

"Are you okay, Dad?"

"Yeah, just gimme a minute."

A few moments passed, then he opened his eyes again. "I just wanted to tell you that I've been a damned fool, and I'm sorry. I know I drove you away with all my talk, and I hope you can forgive me. I've been doing a lot of thinking lately, and

I know we need to talk more about this. But not like before. No more yelling and condemning."

"It's okay. If you really mean what you're saying now, I forgive you."

"Thank you, Matty. Your Mama can tell you what's been going on. I need to sleep right now, but I'll talk to you later."

Matthew turned to his mom, and she led him out of the room.

Neil saw movement in his peripheral vision and looked up to find Matthew and his mom walking down the hall arm in arm. Matthew was shaking his head, and Viola was talking to him quietly.

"Is everything okay?" Neil stood as they approached.

"Yeah. Dad says he'll be fine, and Mom agrees. But I'm also more confused than ever." He turned toward Viola, "Mom, what was Dad talking about?"

"That's gonna take a bit to explain. But since visiting hours are just about over, why don't we go home; I'll fix something to eat and tell you everything."

"Okay, but just so you know, Neil's coming with us."

"That's fine. Let me go say good night to your father, and then we can leave."

After she left, Neil said, "What happened?"

"I'm not really sure. Dad just said he'd been a damned fool and asked me to forgive him. I can't remember the last time I heard my dad curse. I guess we're all gonna find out soon."

"Are you sure you want me there? I mean, this is a family

thing, right? I can get a hotel somewhere nearby if that's easier."

"No way," Matthew said sternly. "You said it before; we're doing this together. I want you there with me."

MATTHEW AND NEIL were sitting around the dining room table at the Palmer home. It was Early American in decor and quite cozy. Viola had put a couple of containers of frozen beef stew into the microwave to thaw and was making a salad to accompany it.

She transferred the thawed stew to a large Dutch oven. Then she joined them at the table. Just then, the door opened, and Marcus and Micah entered, carrying a few bottles of red wine.

"We don't drink much in this house anymore, but I thought some wine might be a good idea tonight," Viola said. "Micah, be a dear and get the wine glasses out of the hutch, please."

While Micah retrieved the stemware, Marcus opened one of the bottles.

"Some of what your father said earlier is just as much my fault as it was his," Viola began, looking at Matthew. "I realize now how much Reverend Davis affected your dad's thinking, and I didn't do anything to stop it."

"He wasn't so bad when he first came to our church several years ago. But ever so slowly, he started condemning things. Looking back, I can see now that he was subtle about it, but it continued, and he slowly got people to think the same way he did."

"I never did like him," Matthew admitted. "He always seemed to have an agenda about something. Mostly about things that were important to me."

"Well, I got sucked in with the rest of the congregation, I'm sorry to say. Maybe not to the same degree as some of them—like your father, for instance—but we were all taken in by his charm."

"So what changed, Mama? Why is Dad apologizing now?"

"Eight months ago, Reverend Davis took a sabbatical from our church to do some missionary work. I don't believe it was his idea originally, but I don't know for sure. I'm not very good friends with most of the congregation, but there were rumors that he was encouraged to step away for a little while.

"Anyway, we got a new minister to fill in for him. Reverend Latham turned out to be a blessing in so many ways. His style of preaching is completely different from Reverend Davis. He spoke of love and caring and acceptance. It affected your father very strongly. I think he realized, as many of us did, that we'd been led astray by Reverend Davis and his teachings." Viola got up to check on the pot of stew.

"Your dad has been thinking a lot about everything, but he was still struggling some with all the information floating around in his brain. You don't erase years of teaching with just a few months of listening to Reverend Latham. But I'll give him this, he was trying. Just a couple of weeks ago, he told me that he was wrong about you, and he needed to fix that."

"Wow." Matthew sighed. "I don't know what to say."

"All I ask, Matty, is that you give him some time. In many ways, he's still processing this information. He's trying to figure it all out."

Viola served up stew for each of them and once she was

seated again held out her hands. They all joined hands as she said grace.

As they ate, their conversation shifted to other things.

"So how was the cruise?" Marcus asked.

"It was amazing," Matthew said, smiling at his brother. "Like nothing I've ever experienced before. I'll show you pictures later."

"The stew is delicious, Mrs. Palmer," Neil said.

"Thank you, Neil. And please, call me Viola." Pausing, she gave Neil a measured look before continuing. "Now, is there something I should know about you and my son?"

"Um ...," Neil began, unsure of what exactly to say.

"Yes, Mama," Matthew said. "Neil and I are dating. It's fairly new, but we're both serious about this and want to see where it leads."

"Okay, then." She looked at Neil. "I can see how you look at him and also how he looks at you. I can't say I understand it all, but I'm willing to try."

"Thank you, ma'am. I care about your son very much and will do anything I can to make sure he's happy."

THE NEXT DAY, Matthew and Neil visited the hospital to see Matthew's dad. Viola and Matthew's brothers were coming along later. After hours of conversation the night before and that morning, Matthew had decided that he would head back to Westport with Neil that day.

He was still processing what his mom had told him about the goings on with Reverend Davis but was sure that eventually he'd be able to forgive his dad. It would take time, but they could get through it.

"I'll wait out here," Neil said, pointing at the waiting area. "I've got my Kindle to keep me occupied."

"Okay, I won't be long."

"Take all the time you need."

His dad was looking out the window. He smiled when he saw Matthew in the doorway.

"Hello, Matty. I almost thought I was dreaming yesterday when I saw you."

"Hi, Dad. I'm really here. I've got to get back home today, but I wanted to stop by and see you before I left. Mama told me about what's been going on with Reverend Davis and now Reverend Latham."

Dad sighed. "I can't tell you how sorry I am, son. But I also have to tell you that I'm still trying to figure some things out. I can't say that I'm thrilled about your life or lifestyle or whatever, but I'm trying. It's just gonna take me some time."

"I get it, Dad. I'm still hurt by everything that's happened between us, but if we can talk through it all, I think we're gonna be okay."

"That's all I ask, son."

"How are you feeling today?"

"Better than I have the past couple of days. I saw my cardiologist this morning, and he said they'll most likely let me go home tomorrow."

"That's great! Mama will be so happy. She, Marcus, and Micah will be here in a little while. I think she wanted to give me some time alone with you."

"Yep, that sounds like your mama." He chuckled.

"So like I said, I've gotta get on the road. I've … um, well, the thing is, I've got a friend here with me, and he's flying home to Washington, DC tomorrow, so I need to get him back to my friend Rob's today."

"A friend, hmmm? Something about the way you said that makes me think he's maybe more than a friend?"

"Honestly, we've just starting dating, but I really think he could be the one, Dad." Matthew's heart was pounding. It felt weird to talk to his dad about his boyfriend and not be yelled at.

"Do you think maybe I could meet him before you leave?"

"Oh, um, sure. I'll go get him."

Matthew hurried out of the room and headed straight for Neil.

"Neil, c'mon. My dad wants to meet you."

"Huh? Really?"

"Yeah, I kinda told him about us. Let's go." Neil looked shocked, but he followed Matthew.

They entered the room together, and Matthew said, "Dad, I'd like you to meet my boyfriend, Neil."

His dad reached out his hand. "Hi, Neil. It's very nice to meet you. I'm Mitchell, but everyone calls me Mitch."

"Very pleased to meet you, sir."

Now that the ice was broken, they chatted for a while. Finally, Mitch said, "Well, I don't want to keep you boys any longer. I know you need to get back to Westport. And frankly, I'm feeling like a nap before your mama gets here."

As they were walking to the car, Matthew took Neil's hand.

"Well, that certainly went a lot better than I ever expected.

I've got a good feeling about this." He lifted their joined hands. "I'm so happy I decided to take that cruise."

"Me, too, sweetheart. Me too."

EPILOGUE

"We're lucky Sam was able to find a deal for your flight, sweetheart." Neil was so excited that he'd finally see Matthew in person the next day.

"I know, right?" Matthew smiled broadly on the FaceTime call. They were both sitting up in bed, catching up on the day's activities. "I don't know how she does it, but I'm grateful that she wields that travel magic. I sent you my flight details, right?"

"Yeah, I added them to my calendar. I'm picking up my rental car at lunchtime, and I'll pick you up at the airport. I'll text you once I know the make and color of the SUV so you can look for me when you leave baggage claim."

Sure, a long-distance relationship was somewhat challenging, but they'd both discovered that they wanted this to work so were willing to put in the extra effort. It had been two months since they were together on the cruise and then in New Hampshire. They fell into a routine where they texted daily and video chatted a few times a week, including some sexy ones. And of course, there were random phone calls mixed in for good measure. In November, Neil had sent flowers to Matthew to commemorate their one-month anniversary, and Neil had received a package at the office containing a framed selfie of the two of them that Matthew had taken when they were on Mykonos. It now sat proudly in a place of honor on Neil's desk.

"How are your folks doing?" Neil asked. Matthew's dad had slowed his life down after the heart attack and was now officially semiretired from the architectural firm where he worked. "Were they upset that you weren't going to spend Christmas with them?"

"They're both well. Dad's not thrilled about not working full-time, but Mama's firm about him taking it easy. And they both understood that I had made Christmas plans with you before we started mending our fences."

"Okay, good. I don't want to cause a rift between the three of you just as you're starting to rebuild that relationship."

"It's fine," Matthew assured him. "Both of my parents really like you, so they're not upset. I told them I'll go up to visit in early January, and we'll have a small Christmas celebration then."

"Really? They like me?" Neil shook his head in disbelief.

"Of course. Why wouldn't they?"

"I dunno. It's always difficult to know for sure. And we didn't meet under the best circumstances, with your dad in the hospital and everything."

"They've both said that they think you're good for me—

not exactly sure what they mean by that, but I *know* you're good for me, so I'm not gonna ask." Matthew chuckled.

"Yeah, you're pretty good for me too, love," Neil said tenderly. "Oh, before I forget, Kyle invited us over for an early dinner tomorrow night. He and Jon are leaving Saturday morning to spend Christmas with Ben and Rob in Westport, so this will be a little Christmas celebration for just the four of us."

"Oh, good." Matthew's face lit up. "I was hoping I'd get to see them before Christmas."

Neil yawned. "Sorry, love, but I'm beat."

"No apologies necessary, sweetheart. Sleep well, and I'll see you tomorrow." Matthew blew him a kiss.

"Love you," replied Neil as he ended the call.

Tuesday, December 27, Wytheville, VA

"OUR FIRST CHRISTMAS TOGETHER," Matthew sighed. "I had a really great time with your family." They'd spent a long weekend with Neil's mom, sister, and her family. There had been lots of food, drink, and laughs in addition to presents on Christmas morning.

"I'm so glad you were able to come with me," said Neil. "And they all really like you. Mom took me aside at one point and said she's never seen me happier. She thinks you are, and I quote, 'the one.'"

"What? She actually said that? Wow." Matthew felt his stomach flutter.

"Yeah, so I guess you're stuck with me." Neil chuckled.

"Works for me, but of course that means you're stuck with me too."

"I think I can manage." Neil reached out and took Matthew's hand. "I love you, you know."

"And I love you." Matthew smiled. "We're gonna make this work, you know."

"Oh, I know. Now I haven't had a chance to ask you yet, but have you had time to talk with Sam about a weekend getaway to Hawthorne Bluff in the spring?" Ever since Ben and Rob had told them about their mini vacation before the wedding, they'd been thinking about visiting the Massachusetts coastal town.

"Yeah, I mentioned it to her, and she promised to check availability at the B&B based on the times you'd be able to take off from work."

They spent most of the five-hour trip back to DC discussing their long-distance life together. Matthew just knew that this was going to work out for both of them. He could feel it in his bones. Who knew when they agreed to join Rob and Ben and the rest of their family and friends on that spectacular cruise that he and Neil would end up finding love in the Mediterranean?

The End

A Letter from RJ

Dear Reader,

Thank you so much for reading Love in the Mediterranean. The next book in this series is Love is for Family. When a devastating family tragedy occurs, Kyle and Jon must suddenly find themselves caring for Kyle's nephew, Wyatt. As a result, their still new relationship faces challenges more quickly than they planned. But they survived because, love is really all about family.

Be sure to follow me on Amazon to be notified of new releases, and look for me on Facebook for sneak peeks of upcoming stories.

Please take a moment to write a review of Love in the Mediterranean on Amazon and Goodreads. Reviews can make all the difference in helping a book show up in Amazon searches.

To to sign up for my newsletter, stop by rj-peterson.ck.page.

We have a great reader group on Facebook that can be found here: www.facebook.com/groups/rjpetersonsadventurers/

Finally, several of my titles are available on audio, narrated by the amazing Kevin Earlywine or the fabulous Cole Kurtz. They can be found here: link.rjpeterson.net/audio

Happy reading!

RJ

P.S. Keep going for a free download!

FREE SHORT STORY

Download a copy of His Elevator Pitch

Inspired by a writing prompt, His Elevator Pitch is the story of River, an unemployed executive assistant, and Thom, the department head of a prestigious multi-faceted corporation.

When a power failure takes out several city blocks in Boston, MA, they find themselves stuck in an elevator with nothing but time on their hands.

Conversation ensues and when power is restored, River goes off to his interview, thinking that's the end of his encounter with the handsome stranger. Or is it?

This story features many of the themes my writing is known for: older guys, sweet-with-heat encounters, low or no angst, and always a happily ever after.

SCAN THE CODE TO DOWNLOAD

About the Author

Hi, I'm RJ! I'm a retired graphic designer. An avid reader—preferably while sipping a vodka martini or bourbon on the rocks—I've had a long and varied career, including library page, car wash attendant, travel agent, and graphic designer in the marijuana industry. In addition, I worked in the banking industry for twenty-five years. I love to travel and have been on 60+ cruises. When not on a cruise, my husband & I live in New England.

I never planned to be a writer, but a fateful day in January, 2021 changed it all. I woke with a story stuck in my head and started typing. The more I type, the more story ideas I get.

Find all my links here:

WANT TO READ MORE?

The New Adventures in Love Series:

Love On The Horizon

Love For The Holidays

Love On The Potomac

Love In The Mediterranean

Love Is For Family

(Coming in 2025)

Hawthorne Bluff Series:

Finding Finlay

Addicted to Ashton

Chasing Courtland

(Coming in 2026)

SEAsons of Love Series:

Love at Frost Sight

Resting Grinch Face

Don't Claus a Scene

Great Chemis-Tree